to Sam

First published in 2021 by Henningham Family Press
130 Sandringham Road, London, E8 2HJ
henninghamfamilypress.co.uk

Illustrations © David Henningham, 2021

Typeset by the author

Printed and bound by T J Books Ltd, Padstow
& Henningham Family Press, London

ISBN   9781916218635

Supported using public funding by
ARTS COUNCIL
ENGLAND
LOTTERY FUNDED

Pupa

J. O. MORGAN

HENNINGHAM
FAMILY
PRESS

EARLY PHASE

1 · SAL

The room had been painted black: the floorboards, the radiators, the plywood nailed over the windows. Everything was black. The hazy press of air was warm and wet. The walls dripped. Their blackness glistened in the pale light coming from the pods—five fat chrysalids hanging heavy from the ceiling. The pods glowed faintly, a soft grey light issuing from the wide membranous gaps between darker mottlings.

The boy edged closer, his lips pressed tightly closed, his short breaths hissing thinly through his nose. The pods swelled before him. They were as big as he was. A muddle of thick gluey fibres connected each one to the ceiling. They swayed now gently, as though the boy's step had disturbed them, as though their drooping bulk was minutely sensitive to any slight shift in the room's humid cube of air.

The darker patches on the pods were golden, a fine metallic lustre through which the inner glow was unable to pass. The gold was perfectly curved, smoothed from the press of each interior.

The boy raised his bare arm towards the nearest chrysalis, his skin as pale as the light that came from deep inside the pod, his arm glowing, just as the pod glowed, becoming ever more translucent the closer he came to touching that taut outer membrane.

He brushed the back of his hand against the coolness of the gold, trailing his fingers over the brittle shell-like substance and onto the softness of the glowing grey. He felt a gentle warmth there. It was like skin. It was like his skin, smooth and pale and papery, yielding to the softness of his outstretched fingertips.

A new wetness made him draw his hand away. A single drip was forming on one side of the pod. It grew from where the boy's last touch had been. He examined his hands in the dim light, feeling round the curve of his black fingernails, finding the tiny jagged edge that had snagged on the pod's papery surface.

The misty drip grew without falling. It was a smooth white seed, a glossy dew drop pushing out from the skin. A pinpoint of brightness was visible within it, centring the spot at which the boy's nail had punctured the membrane.

The brightness increased. It extended into a downward split, at first no more than a single silk-thin line of milky light. Then with a low wet moan the split widened, allowing the contents of the chrysalis to pour unhesitatingly through it. A thick pale lumpy liquid, forcing the gap open by its sudden unsupported weight. In one long gush it spilled out onto the black floor and spread, splashing up against the black walls, pooling around the boy's feet, oozing warm between his bare grey toes.

Somewhere in the building an alarm began to sound, a shrill broken chiming—repetitive, insistent.

The empty skin of the chrysalis hung limp from the cords still holding it to the ceiling. No light now came from within it. The glow of the newly spilled liquid was already fading.

•

Sal opened his small black eyes. He was lying on his back in the dark. The phone continued ringing downstairs. He rose to answer it.

A faint flicker came from the end of the stair as Sal descended. There was no light on in the house. Old man

Madox was still sitting in his armchair in the lounge, the crest of his thin bald head showing above the line of the armchair's high back, his pale grey skin reflecting in flickers the blizzard of light that came from the television screen. The phone lay on a low table not far behind him but Madox made no move to silence it.

Sal hesitated, waiting for another long ring to begin before swiftly lifting the receiver.

'Yes?'

There was a brief pause before he heard the voice. He recognised it at once.

'Sal? I know, it's early. You know how these things can be. But if you want to get a good look. While it's all still fresh.'

'Yes?'

'I only just got the call myself. About to set out now. Should be fine for you to come along.'

'What is it? I'll have to be at work.'

'Usual thing. Break-in. Sounds like a real mess though. You okay to come take a peek? Drop you at work straight after.'

'I don't like being late.'

'You won't be. But of course if you're not interested, it's no matter. Someone else may be. And one of these will surely turn up some other time—or similar. I'm not fussed either way.'

'No. I'm interested. I'm up. I need a while to get ready.'

'What you need is permission from your father.'

Sal glanced at the figure in the armchair. The shiny dome of head had not yet moved, the wash of screen-light still shimmering over it.

'He says that's fine. Yes. He's nodding.'

'Fifteen minutes.'

'Here?'

'*Right outside.*'

Sal opened his mouth to reply but the call had already been cut. He listened to the hum a moment more before lowering the receiver.

The television's faint flicker of light caught on the back of Sal's hand. He gazed down at it blankly: the marbled grey skin, the long featureless digits, the absent fingernails.

Sal sat leaning slightly forward in the passenger seat. He was in his work clothes, an off-white shirt with narrow charcoal tie and matching slacks. Over this he wore a thin waterproof, his small round head poking from the raised collar just as old Madox's had stuck up above the back of the chair, smooth and bald and blue-grey.

There was a scent of perfume in the car. It was faint but Sal could feel its sharp chemical bite washing round him. If the perfume was on the leather headrest, even just a smear, he didn't want it on his skin. He tried to keep his breathing shallow.

'You can relax if you like. We're not in any hurry.'

The inspector's voice was deep and assured. Sal's was not.

'I prefer sitting this way.'

On his lap Sal held his veg-box, his fingers gripping the plastic clip-seal sides. Within was mostly lettuce, the bruised leaves pressed down so that Sal could fit more in. Along with this was half a cucumber and two small tomatoes. Sal had to be careful with tomatoes; he liked them, but too many could upset his simple gut.

The sky was still dark. The streetlamps pulsed slowly into the car as it cruised the empty roads, the misty plastic of the veg-box glowing and fading in response.

'The car's fine, Sal. You know I wouldn't do that to you. I made sure the garage used a neutral wash.'

The inspector was dark-skinned, his soft bronze-brown hair cut short, neatly combed and oiled flat. His eyes were green. Over a dark brown suit he wore a long leather raincoat. The leather was supple; highly burnished. It had the deep mottled colour of a ripe plum, complete with bluish overtint. When the coat caught the light from the streetlamps a yellow glow would flicker over the leather's smooth creases in little bright lines from cuff to shoulder, before the coat was abruptly cast into shadow again.

'I know, Mr Augustine. I know you wouldn't.' Sal maintained his rigid position. 'I like sitting this way. It's comfortable. I prefer it.'

The inspector smiled and shrugged.

A few silent streets further on and the car pulled up in front of a residential block. There were no lights to be seen through the many windows. The front door was open, an unlit corridor beyond.

'We had reports of a disturbance. An upper apartment. We often get such calls.' Augustine slipped from the car and stood leaning back against it, studying the old building, waiting for Sal to extract himself from his seat. 'I think sometimes they do it out of fear it may someday be true. This one seemed genuine enough. I've a way of testing—a little trick I thought up.'

As they went on in the inspector examined the door for signs of forced entry. There was a large ragged gap where the handle and lock should have been. The breaks were not fresh, being wet and flecked with fine white mould; the door itself hooked back against the wall.

Augustine clicked on a small pocket torch.

'So, you see, this lady, the caller, she sounded scared, right? They often do. So I ask her to go and take a closer look. She says not a chance. Fair enough. But then I ask for her own door number. That's the trick, see. If she says no to this, well, then I say I'm sorry but I can't come out. I mean it too. But if she relents and gives it then, okay, it's usually worth the trip—usually.'

The inspector came to a halt and knocked gently at one of the apartments. There was a shuffle from behind the door. The pin of light visible in the spyhole was briefly blackened. The door stayed shut. It would be too dark in the hallway for them to be seen clearly. The inspector knocked again.

'Hello, Madam? I understand you put in a call?'

He put his mouth closer to the doorframe, his head lowered. He had no intention of shouting.

'My name's Inspector Augustine. We spoke earlier.'

No answer.

'About a commotion upstairs?'

His soft deep voice. Its easy calm tone.

'You don't need to come out. You don't even need to speak. I just need a few details.'

Another shuffling sound. A pause. A scrape of paper.

The torch was angled downwards to where a white square protruded from under the door. The inspector snatched it up without further comment and he and Sal moved off towards the stairwell.

The handle and lock of the apartment they'd come to examine had been bashed through in a similar way to that of the lower door, but the breakage here was dry. Sharp splinters still protruded. There was yellow dust on the floor.

The door swung back at a gentle push. Augustine put on the light as they entered.

The main room was bare but for an old couch along one wall and two small crates of tinned food stacked beside it. The opposite corner was a mess. A clutch of broken egg-cases. They were white and leathery, each about the size of a man's clenched fist. A thick pink goo had spread from what remained of their floppy shells.

'Nothing all that unusual.' The inspector crouched beside them. 'Eggs get abandoned. Eggs get discovered. Eggs get destroyed.' He shrugged. 'Still have to carry out an inspection, though. Still have to write it all up.' He counted the eggs, tapping what remained of each one with the end of his pen. 'All this just because some folk don't like hatchlings in their neighbourhood.' He took a length of measuring tape from his pocket and made a guess at the original dimensions of each shell, writing the details in his pocketbook. 'Then again, maybe it was for food—or else for kicks.'

'The tins are all still in their crate.'

Sal bent forward to twist one round beneath its tight plastic wrap. The label was still partly obscured. Some sort of meaty broth. Sal let go.

'For kicks then.' Augustine rubbed his nose. 'Though the tins wouldn't be for the hatchlings. They'd not know what they were, let alone how to get into them. And whoever did this wouldn't be interested in that sort of food. Not to eat, at any rate.'

The inspector took photographs of the broken eggs, a small silver camera in one hand, his other holding out the flash box on a springy length of flex.

'Not many of these hatchlings survive anyway. Not on their own. If there's no one about then the stronger eat the weaker till only one is left. We're all the same at that age. You. Me. We probably ate our siblings before we were discovered. Alone, new born, holding death at bay by dishing it out.'

Sal glanced at the mess of eggs, at the misty pinkness that had congealed into a stiff puddle around the disfigured white shells. He squeezed his podgy fingers into fists.

'What if they're never found?'

'Oh, they'd be screeching by that time. They get found. Destroying fresh eggs is one thing. You could argue they're not yet really alive. But destroying a newborn? A fully-formed larval? Tiny and hungry and howling? Not many would want to risk that. Risk being found out, I mean. And fostering does pay. A little. Enough.'

The inspector stood smoothly then stepped aside through the dark doorway of an adjoining room.

Sal stayed where he was.

A tatty magazine stuck out from the base of the crates. Sal tugged at it till it came free. It was a clothing catalogue. Only a few months out of date. Well-thumbed. There were page corners folded down. Select items had been circled.

Sal clenched his jaw, staring at nothing, his voice a dreamy murmur, little more than a hum upon his lips.

'I'm happy just as I am.'

He rolled the catalogue tight, tucking it inside his waterproof.

And all the while Inspector Augustine stood watching him, intently, from the deep dark of the adjoining room, saying nothing, merely observing, knowing how he couldn't himself be seen.

3 . MEGAN

Sal sat bowed at his desk, his small black eyes moving between the number-pad over which his right hand hovered and the sheet of figures where his left hand marked position. There was an orderly bustle and hum beyond the thin white walls of his cubicle: the mixed activity of all the other office workers, each of them just as busy as he was. Occasional changes in light and shadow could be marked through the misty plastic of the partitions, when anyone passed near enough.

Sal was aware of both the humming and the motion, though he never looked up nor paused in his work. The sounds and the movements were comforting. He felt fully part of the office environment. An equal part. The tapping on his keypad itself added to that mingled office noise. The short side-to-side motion of his head aided in the collective forward motion of all office work.

He was archiving. He didn't know what he was archiving. He wasn't required to know. He knew only that it was necessary. A continuing process within the workplace. Within every workplace.

A neat stack of printouts lay on his desk. Each page contained several columns of figures. Sal entered those figures into his machine, working one narrow column at a time, one finger of his left hand holding place while his right hand tapped in each individual number.

He worked slowly. The figures would be entered with perfect accuracy. Sal's head swayed, his tight little mind moving from one hand to the other, picking up the number-line and carrying its memory over to the hand that worked the machine. The freshly input figures glowed orange on the small square screen above the keypad, but Sal never looked up. He would retain the information in his head only for as long as was required. He could tell it was correct in the very moment of its transferral. There was no need for him, nor anyone else, to check.

The office had to retain paper copies for six months. Then the archived data had to be kept for a further three years. The information was not routinely accessed, but it needed to be available for anyone who might at some point find it necessary to look. Sal made sure this potential need was satisfied. He made sure the information was reliable.

The blurred shape of his colleague in the neighbouring cubicle drummed upon the soft partition wall. Sal carried on with his work. The shape stood, came round into Sal's cubicle, and placed another stack of papers beside the one already there. Sal made no move to acknowledge the girl standing beside him. He continued slowly down the column of figures. The data was keyed in.

Megan watched till the tip of Sal's finger was at the last figure but one.

'Ready now?'

She didn't wait for an answer. She went back to her own cubicle and rolled her heavy chair round to sit beside him. The papers Sal had been working on were duly shifted to the corner of his desk. The numeric keypad was folded back into the machine.

'Take half.'

Megan roughly divided the stack. Boxes of clips were taken from one of Sal's desk drawers, envelopes from another. Each letter in the stack had to be signed, the two pages clipped together, the paper folded twice, enveloped, sealed, placed to one side.

'I don't understand why he would show you that.'

Megan laid everything out carefully before getting to work; each necessary item placed within easy reach.

'Why would he wake you so early in the morning and drive you out to such a place and show you that? Was it to scare you? It shouldn't be allowed. Were you scared? Maybe he's right. These things do happen, I suppose. Did it make you feel sick? You could make a complaint. Why do you even like him? Do you even like him? What's he like?'

They had special tools for folding the paper. Their pale grey skin was too dry and would tear if they used only their fingers. The tools were smooth flat lengths of animal bone. It would not melt with the friction of folding. It would leave no ugly mark on the paper.

'I don't mind.' Sal examined the end of his folder, feeling for its smoothest, most rounded edge. 'I wanted to go. He shows me things. He knows my father. He knows me. I find it interesting. Those things he shows me.'

Megan worked through her stack methodically. She liked to do all the signing and clipping in one go, making a new stack as she went. Then she'd go back through the new stack for folding and enveloping.

'And the hatchlings eat each other? That can't be true. It's barbaric. We weren't taught that. I don't believe that. Why would they choose not to teach us that? I suppose it's not something anyone wants to know. I don't think I'd want to know. Is it really what happens?'

Sal preferred to work letter by letter. He would sign, clip, fold, stuff and seal the envelopes one letter at a time, each finished and laid neatly to one side before the next was begun.

'I think I knew. I'm not sure how. I don't remember it. Better not to remember. It's just the way of things. You probably did it too. You survived.'

A supervisor stood unnoticed behind them. A woman with thick blonde curls, dressed finely in a mauve trouser suit. She watched the two larvals for a while, following their slow progress down through the letter-stack. Then, having made a few brief notes on her clipboard, she moved quietly away.

'But you don't actually know that. You can't prove it. It's disgusting. Maybe I was discovered early. I might have been lucky that way. Or maybe that's why those eggs were destroyed. Who'd want that going on next door to them? There must be some who are more caring. More tolerant. There ought to be rules against it. There should be whole systems in place to prevent this sort of thing.'

A flicker of shadow over the letters made Megan turn her head. Another worker was passing the narrow entrance to the cubicle: another bald-headed larval like them, pushing a paper-laden trolley. The office hum continued unabated. Megan went back to her work.

'Do you really think it makes much of a difference? The thicker skin? All that hair? It can't be just to keep them warm. I'm always warm. Do you think it would feel nice? It does look very soft. There must be other benefits. Else why go through all that palaver. Would you? It must be worth the risk. I think. Maybe.'

Sal stopped and stared at her for a moment. His small black eyes watching as she busily, eagerly, folded sheet after sheet and placed them to one side. When he spoke he did so in a calm flat tone.

'There are no benefits. There's nothing to be gained. I'm happy just as I am.'

Megan did not return his look. She didn't seem to notice. She went right on with her folding.

Sal looked away. He signed another letter. He reached for his box of clips.

Sal gazed openly at his father across the dinner table. He watched the old man's pale, near-translucent face hanging forward over the wide grey bowl, the lower jaw drawing its heavy circles as he chewed to a fine purée anything he put into the slowly revolving machinery of his mouth.

Sal knew this man couldn't really be his father. He'd known it from as long ago as he could recall understanding such things. Then he'd forgotten about it. There had been no need to consider it any further. It was the same circumstance with any larval he'd ever known. And yet, having seen the broken eggs that morning, having stood so close to the congealed mess that had been so simplistically halted in its process of becoming something more solid, something more tangible—

Madox couldn't be anyone's father, being no less of a larval than Sal himself. He was merely old. Old and tall and thin. He'd never pushed himself to make that change. He'd never had the desire to do so.

The kitchen light had been pulled low on its extension cable, its bright white circle fixed within the limits of the table's own circular rim. In the other room the television was on, its sound up, the tin-voiced narration interrupting the various clicks and hisses and rasps.

'...*newly emerged female adult, having dried and hardened will soon seek out food and, being exhausted from her necessary fasting of many days, will gorge on whatever she can find, including…'*

The cone of light was so bright it penetrated the greyness of Madox's smooth bald head, revealing the shadowed latticework of blueish bone beneath. If Madox were to lift his face Sal might even have seen the food being mashed between his father's dark chitinous gums.

'…on into adulthood and sexual maturity, with all the eggs she will ever lay already formed, dormant within her, each one a single tight cell, they too requiring nourishment to be stimulated into further development, whereupon…'

They were eating warm parsnip soup. Sal had left his unseasoned. No spices. No salt. Even his finely cut lengths of carrot had been carefully peeled and washed for him to suck at, with Sal occasionally snapping off pieces small enough to swallow.

Madox ate his carrots skin and all, stringy root-tips and knotty heads, along with whatever greenery was still sticking out. He even ate the peel and stubby tops and tails that Sal left in a tangled heap at the edge of his plate.

'…beyond a certain threshold, thereby attaining full fertility, and in so doing she becomes irresistible to any unwitting male who, having followed her scent line, and having then proved his own suitability through an intricate series…'

As he watched his father Sal winced to imagine those flecks of earth, the grit housed in the knobbly roughness of the peel. He imagined the sudden crunch of the tiny grains between Madox's gums. He imagined them between his own gums. He imagined the quick scrape of each particle against the softness of that long throat as they went down. It made him shiver. It made him look away.

'...*may then be permitted to mount the female, doing so at first with great delicacy and trepidation, though the surety of their embrace is very soon reinforced by the male's powerful forward pincers, which now he squeezes around the back of his mate's...*'

Up in his room, with the noise from the downstairs television still reaching thinly through the floor, Sal dug under his pillow and slid out the clothing catalogue he'd taken that morning.

It was not meant for the likes of him. This was adult clothing. Colourful. Elegant. Expensive. He turned the pages slowly, his head bowed, the bright black spots of his eyes examining the faces of the models, their fixed expressions of blank contentment, their long glossy hair, their sleek dark skin and visible musculature, the carefree poses continuing changeless through the catalogue, the lessening number of clothes being worn, the contoured bulging of their underwear.

'...*despite this the organ itself is little more than a fine transparent tube, a connecting pipe which, when fully unravelled, he feeds precariously into the female, reinforcing the need for him to hold her perfectly still, for at this point any sudden motion on her part could...*'

Sal laid the catalogue to one side and unbuttoned his work trousers, sliding them forward over his narrow blue-grey thighs. He glanced at the catalogue, then back at himself. He traced his spongy fingertips over the empty area between his legs, pressing every so often gently inward towards the base of his gut. But he found no hint of anything beneath the smooth mistiness of his skin. There was no change in the inner softness of the tissue, not even the suggestion of a bump. Nothing there but the small familiar hole at his torso's lowest point. A single neat aperture through which anything not wanted by his body was expelled.

'...*prompts the necessity for a secure location, for though the duration of fluid transferral may in itself be brief, the two may stay locked together in this manner for several hours, dissuading rival males over such a period from any attempt at*...'

Downstairs the television was switched off.

Sal sat suddenly upright.

He could hear old Madox talking. A raspy mumbling. And there was a second voice. A softer deeper voice.

Sal hadn't heard anyone arriving. The bell hadn't been rung. He pulled up his trousers and rebuttoned them, shoving the catalogue back under his pillow before soft-stepping to his bedroom door and easing it open.

The two men weren't talking particularly quietly. Their words weren't hushed. Nevertheless Sal crept only a short way down the staircase to where the shade of the upstairs landing ceased, sitting himself upon the last darkened step.

Both men were seated in opposite armchairs in front of the television. The television itself had not in fact been turned off, merely muted. The channel had been switched, the greens of the documentary giving way to the glaring blues and pinks of a daily gameshow.

Old Madox glanced at the screen from moment to moment while the two men talked, though his tone when he did speak as ever stayed slow and level.

'He doesn't want things to change. It doesn't interest him. He told me so. He likes things as they are. We like it this way. We always have.'

The other man was Inspector Augustine. He sat forward in his chair with eager intent, his forearms rested on his knees.

'And yet he's certainly interested. You can't deny that. He enjoys our little outings. And I would never force the boy. But there's surely no harm in him taking an interest. No?'

'He can do what he likes. I don't mind.' Madox had gazed away once again. 'It won't lead anywhere.'

Augustine settled back in his seat. He picked at the worn fabric of his armrest.

'That's not really for you to say.'

'He says it himself. He's happy as he is.'

'But the opportunity. The potential. It's there for him nonetheless. You must acknowledge that. And help can always be provided. If you see what I mean. One really does need help in these matters. Good guidance.' He smiled. The expression went unnoticed. 'So there'd be no risk. He'd not be alone. Not at all. So many choose to do these things alone. You know, in secret. Such a poor choice. Unnecessary. That's really where the problems start.'

'He isn't alone.' Madox directed his words at the television. 'There won't be any risk. He's—'

'Yes, I know. *He's happy as he is.* Of course. I understand that. As you yourself are.' The inspector smiled
warmly, sincerely. 'And nothing wrong in that. Not at
all. I'm glad of it. I thank you for it.'

Madox gave no answer, staring as he was at the screen
all the while: the larval contestants, lined lumpily behind
their electronic columns; the glamorous adult host with
her stack of cards, moving between them, laying her
hand upon their backs as she bent in to talk.

'Choice. That's what it comes down to. That's all I
want to impress upon the boy. A sense of choice. That
such an avenue is, at least, open to him. And always will
be. I don't mean to tell him so directly. That's no use in
itself.'

'He already knows. He's—'

'He knows, yes, of course, for sure. But I want him to
feel it. To really understand it. That sense of safety. Of—'
Augustine gave a vague hand gesture. 'Of reassurance.
That's all.' The hand flopped back to the chair.

'Only he can choose what he feels.'

The inspector frowned briefly. 'Not sure I follow your
logic there. But he's a reasonably bright boy. Observant
too. In fact, I'm sure he's probably listening to us this
very moment. Sal? Why don't you come in here and join
our little conversation.'

The inspector had turned his head sharply in the
direction of the stairs. He stayed that way, smiling
through two rooms and up towards the shadow under
which the boy was crouched.

Sal tensed, clenching his jaw, holding the pressure.

He felt himself starting to tremble, though he did not move from his spot upon the stair.

Augustine tilted his head as though listening. Then with a short shrug he turned back to face Madox and the two continued their conversation, the television flashing pink and blue between them.

And after a while Sal eased himself from his step and retreated, slowly, up towards his bedroom.

•

The room had been covered all over with thick black paint, its perfume hanging sharp in the fuzziness of the air.

The only light came from a small tumble of pale pink eggs. Each was the size of a man's head. They lay in a sticky cluster, nestled at the room's far corner.

The boy approached cautiously. In his hand he clutched an unopened can of corned beef, the press of his fingers rucking the blue paper label, exposing the tin's hidden key.

Faint shadows moved within the eggs, they squirmed, pushing up against the stiff pink shells, wanting to get out.

The boy knelt before them. He raised the small blunt container to the height of his misty white eyes. With all his strength he brought it down upon the nearest of the eggs.

5 . SILK

Sal and Megan took their lunch breaks together. Their duties were arranged at work to make this possible. They took the break outside in the nearby shopping precinct. They rarely shopped. The shops were meant for others than themselves. More often they wandered, gazing through windows, questioning whatever they might see. It was a means to get away from the office fustiness, out of the stagnant warmth and the faux-comfort of their waxy plastic chairs.

A short walkway ran from the big white-fronted work buildings, between scrubby rectangles of grass, and on into the red-bricked precinct. The pair moved slowly along the path. The midday air was cold. The light was grey. They passed other workers, a little line of folk going forward, a little line going back, all following the narrow walkway as dutifully as they might a taut length of rope. No one ever stepped off onto the grass, though there was nothing to prevent them from doing so.

At the far end of the precinct was a small open area that few people frequented: a dried-up fountain circled by a low stone wall. Here the two larvals sat and ate their lunch. Small boxes were extracted from deep pockets and rested open on their knees.

Megan ate quickly, finishing long before Sal, giving her lunchbox a flick to rid it of moisture and tucking it away once more. She sat now watching him. She waited.

She slipped her knitted cap from her head, turned it floppily in her hands, removed a speck of something as if she were prizing out a thorn, then slipped the cap smoothly on again over her shiny blue-grey skin.

'It's not because I need one. Not really. It's because I want one. Or because I might find one I liked. And anyway, I like to look. Maybe we won't find anything. I hope we do.'

Sal forced a swallow. 'Does it itch?'

'Not this one. No. Some do. If the wool's particularly coarse.'

'I can't wear wool. It feels hot. Each fibre burning. Scorching tiny grooves into my skin.'

The cap Megan wore was old, its colours having faded, its threads having thinned.

'I've had that sort of thing too. A bit. Once. It's fine now. I'm much better with those things now. I think you get used to it. You build up a resistance.'

'I can only wear cotton.'

'That makes sense. Stick with what you're used to. What about silk though? Can you wear silk? I mean, if you actually had some. If you could afford it.'

'Silk's worse. Stings all over. The threads are sharper. They make finer grooves.' Sal wiped out his lunchbox with a cloth then folded the cloth into one pocket of his waterproof and slipped the box into another. 'And I don't like thinking where it comes from. Those huge factories. All that grey sticky web to be harvested.'

'It's not really like that. Not always. Some silk is naturally golden. Some rarer sorts are pink—or pinkish, in the right light. It has to be very carefully farmed and gathered. It's properly done. That's why it's so rare. They have to look after their spiders, you see. They have to feed them up just right.'

'For the most expensive sorts, maybe. If you can trust them. Or maybe they grow it cheap. In secret. Maybe they just tell you it's farmed properly. That the spiders are well treated. Who'd know? Who'd check? All that finely woven web against your skin. Never knowing what went into it. The force-feeding. The dirty little spaces. The unknown diseases.'

'No.' Megan stood. 'Those places are all monitored. They're regulated. Tested. They'd have to be. And it doesn't really matter anyway. I could never afford it.'

She stood waiting, her hands in her pockets.

Sal obediently rose to his feet.

•

The two larvals were the only customers in the clothes shop. A young adult attendant lounged at the front, leaning forward with her elbows on the counter, watching the newcomers. She showed no sign of excluding them. There was nothing to stop them buying or indeed wearing whatever they might like, even if it wouldn't suit their small unshapely bodies.

She smiled at them as they shuffled awkwardly between the low white shelves, keeping close together, murmuring to each other as an item was lifted, gently inspected, then laid back exactly as they'd found it.

At length Megan came forward.

'Hello. We were wondering about silk. We don't want to buy any. We just wondered. Because how do you know, I mean how can you tell, that it's ethically sourced? I know it says so on the labels. I looked. But that's just the labels. How can you really be sure?'

The attendant straightened, finger-combing a thick curtain of dark red hair behind one ear.

'Oh, we can't. Not really. Not for certain.' She shrugged. 'Not without going to the factories ourselves. And not even then. Unless we stayed and watched it being spun and gathered and processed. And then woven and cut and stitched. And then followed it all the way here to the shop.' She smiled. 'But they do have tests. You know, regulations and that. And we trust to those. We have to. But no, we can't be *sure* sure. Not really.'

As Megan and the attendant talked Sal lingered at the rear of the shop. He examined the stacks of neatly folded fabric. The silk felt very soft against his skin. It was like skin itself. It didn't sting when he touched it.

There was a little column of underwear, each layer a thin film to be peeled away. The colours were rich and metallic. Bronze, copper, cobalt, verdigris. There was such a thinness to the fabric that in taking one Sal was able to fold it, over and over, bunching a single garment into a tiny dense triangle of woven silk, small enough to fit within the cushion of his palm. And it was so light. There was hardly anything there. All that expense, for near nothingness.

Sal looked up at the two women. They weren't paying him any attention. They were discussing the business, the attendant answering Megan's many questions, though without any real engagement in the subject. She was much more interested in Megan herself; the brilliant colours of her eyes watching the young larval's every nervous movement.

No hats were discussed, Megan had already seen the prices so there was little point in enquiring, and at length she and Sal left with only a few minutes spare to get back to their office.

•

Once outside the precinct, back on the narrow walkway, Sal slipped his hand from his coat pocket and held it out before Megan. Slowly he opened it to reveal the little balled up pair of silk panties he had chosen not to return to the shelf, the bunched material resettling itself from the hotness of his grip.

Megan stopped walking.

'That's not fair.' She stared at the item, then at Sal. 'You shouldn't take advantage of someone's kindness. She was nice to me. I liked her. Now she'll get in trouble. She'll think we planned it from the start.'

Sal shrugged.

'It won't matter. They have lots.' He looked down at the tiny flop of fabric in his hand. 'And it's only small. They must lose things. Or rip things. They'll be doing that all the time. This won't make any difference.'

He held out his hand to her.

Megan took a corner of the pink coppery softness, letting the fine silk uncrumple soundlessly as she lifted it. A slight breeze was all that was needed to make the silk billow outwards, away from her pinched fingertips.

Without saying another word Megan turned on her heel and ran back towards the shopping complex, clutching tight the stolen item in her fist.

Sal took a few hasty steps after her then stopped.

For a moment he considered calling out, but didn't. He considered how it'd be her now who'd get in trouble. She'd be late back to work. And if he followed her they'd both be late. So he stood and watched her disappear between the buildings, then turned and continued back alone towards the office.

•

It was a long time later when Megan returned to her cubicle, with only the briefest of glances at Sal as she passed. He was hard at work on his archiving. He had said nothing.

Their supervisor came by not long after, looked at them both working, made marks in her chart, and moved on.

Eventually Sal poked his head round the partition wall.

'It wouldn't be fair to blame you. And she got them back. They can't have been ruined. Not that quickly.'

Megan turned slowly to look at him but didn't speak.

'So she should have let you keep them. For your honesty. She could have given you a discount on a new cap. As a reward.'

Still Megan said nothing. She only smiled at him, then turned away, holding the smile as she got on with her work.

6. The Difference

The weekend weather was drizzly.

At the back of the residential area was a scrubby heath that rose gently into a low hill, topped with a spindly copse. A worn mud path was sunk into the slope, bolstered and pegged at intervals by short lengths of timber.

The scrubland itself had no entrance at the near side, only a thin fence, its twin wires unbarbed and untightened, though Sal and Megan still took extra care in ducking under them, keeping the wire's half-rusted surface well clear of their papery skin.

Sal led the way, his head bowed, watching his feet as he and Megan trudged up the damp path. He was grumbling. It was the usual complaint.

'No need to go through such a change. We can already do all that adults do. No need to be anything other than larval.'

Megan nodded even though Sal couldn't see her. She made no attempt to contradict him but her voice was dull, the same old phrases spoken without care.

'I know. You're right. We can. It's so much fuss. Easier like this. And it'd be expensive. It's all so expensive.'

Sal put great effort into climbing each step. Pressing his hands to his knees to give himself support. He was soon out of breath. Still he kept talking.

'And when you end up looking so different, how can

you be sure it's really you? You can't know if you'll like how you'll turn out. And you can't switch back again. That's it forever. You're stuck. At least this way you already know. You can be content. Just as you are.'

Megan matched her steps to Sal's. She watched his shoes, placing hers in just the same spots once he'd lifted his away. She spoke dreamily, repeating his words back to him.

'So different. It's really you. That's it. You already know. You can be. You are.'

There was an old iron bench at the point where the path began to curve around the lower eaves of the copse. The trees drooped over it, the tips of their branches dripping onto the seat.

The bench was cold. Sal wiped away some of the moisture with his sleeve before he and Megan sat, both of them staring down the slope of the heath to the houses. It wasn't much of a view, just the back end of the city, its cramped buildings stretching away into the grey haze of drizzled sky.

'They're not happy. Not really. They can't be.' Sal clenched his jaw. 'That's why they cover up with all those fancy clothes. When they change they feel it's not enough. Then they have to pretend they're happy. Because they know that's all it is. They know it wasn't worth it.'

Megan nodded slowly. She nodded with her whole body, stiff-necked, rocking in her seat, her hands dug deep in the pockets of her coat, attentive as Sal continued.

'And you'd miss it. You'd miss not being what you'd always been. What you knew of yourself.'

He was silent for a while, waiting. But when Megan went on merely rocking in her seat Sal looked at her directly.

'Wouldn't you miss being you? The you you are now?'

Megan shrugged and made a downward shape with her mouth.

'Probably. I don't know. I guess. I don't really think it would matter. You can't ever know. Not really.'

Sal went on watching her.

'You could have kept them. Those panties. You should have. You didn't need to take them back. The shop wouldn't have known.'

'I know, I just, in the moment—'

'Maybe you didn't like them.'

Another long shrug. 'I didn't really look. I liked the colour. I liked how they felt on my skin. I liked—I don't know. They weren't mine. I liked giving them back.'

'What did the lady say?'

But Megan didn't answer. She had stopped rocking. Her body was tight, her face pushing forwards, staring out over the city.

Sal stood abruptly. He stood in front of the bench, his hands on his hips. He breathed in deep and puffed out his chest, gazing thoughtfully up at the thick grey sky. Megan angled her head to look at him. She sat back.

Sal thought for a moment. He thought back to the catalogue. He lifted one leg, placing his foot on the edge of the seat, leaning an elbow against his knee, his chin to the knuckles of his fist, staring wistfully into the woods. Megan smiled a little.

'Don't.' She tugged at his sleeve for him to sit back down. 'It seems all wrong in your old coat. It makes you look—' She squinted. 'It doesn't work.'

Sal sat down with a bump, sitting a little closer to Megan than before. He took a short breath and held it. When he spoke again his voice was quieter. It had a vagueness to it.

'What have you got at the top of your legs?'

Another quizzical stare from Megan, but Sal had not been looking her way when he asked.

Megan tried to dismiss the enquiry.

'The same as anyone else, of course.'

But Sal persisted, still quietly, still without meeting her gaze.

'Is it really the same though? I mean, how can you know for sure? How can you know it's just like me?'

'Sal.' Megan frowned. 'Surely you know. Weren't you taught this at school? I was. Didn't you pay attention?'

Sal stared out over the city.

'I don't remember.'

'Alright.' Megan took a deep breath. 'Well, nothing really. Yes. About the same as you. But, you know, it's not what's on the outside that actually matters but what's underneath. And even then—'

'Yes?'

'Well—just a fatty lump. Or a gap. A clear space. It depends. But nothing much more than that. Not with us, at least. You really ought to know all this.'

'Yes. I sort of remember.' Sal squinted at the ground between his feet. 'I mean, it sounds right. But then I sort of don't remember. Not quite. I think that lesson was rushed. I never got to see.'

'Oh.'

'But I'd like to know. To see.'

'It's really nothing.'

There was silence for a while. Sal was staring out over the city once again when he noticed a movement beside him. Turning he saw Megan undoing the tops of her trousers and pulling them partway down, allowing Sal to get a clear look at what wasn't there.

'You see? Nothing. Just like you.'

Sal leaned towards her, straining his small black eyes in the grey daylight. Then he sat back and undid his own trousers and slid them down a little way just as Megan had done, exposing the same smooth empty patch of skin between his legs.

'Ah, but there, see?' Megan pointed. 'A sort of shadow under your skin? A dark area. That's the gap. The lack. I don't have that.'

Sal bent forward to examine himself but couldn't tell what Megan was referring to.

'Maybe you won't see it. There's not much difference. But with me it's a little paler. Just here under the skin. A sort of bump. A fatty patch.'

Sal looked at her, then back at himself. He couldn't see the bump, but now with himself he thought he could just about detect the shadow of an empty space. He'd never noticed it before. He pressed himself with a fingertip, the soft rubbery flesh resuming its roundness as soon as he let go. He leant over to press Megan in the same place but she smacked his hand away.

Sal looked up at her confused, his fingers stinging from the blow. Then he noticed the pale smear of colour on the back of Megan's hand. A soft brownish colour where her skin should be blue-grey like his.

He pointed.

'What's that?'

Megan began doing herself up. Standing and facing away from him as she did so.

'Let's go home. It's cold here.'

Sal chose not to press the question. He began to button himself up as well.

'You know what they do, don't you? As adults? You know what they get up to?'

'Yes, Sal. I know what they do.'

The two larvals began to walk slowly back down the slope.

'I think that's pretty strange. You have to agree that's pretty strange. Why would they want to do that? Who'd want to do that?'

'Well, they would. That's clear enough.'

They descended the steps in silence after this, Sal following, his footfalls out of step with Megan's.

At the edge of the residential estate they parted ways, Sal watching Megan for a moment more before turning and running off home.

7. A Lack

It was a day like any other. Sal arrived at work promptly, filing in alongside his co-workers, all of them funnelled through the low entrance-slit of the tall white-fronted building.

Sal's cubicle enclosed him, curving smoothly inward at the opening, leaving just a narrow gap, holding his own small space of air, his own small smells. He felt safe there. He knew what he was expected to do and he did it. He tucked his chair close into his desk and set to his routine, switching on each machine in his own preferred order, each new buzz adding to the warmth of aliveness around him, till his whole space was humming, and him held safe at its core.

Only once he was fully settled did Sal hesitate. He glanced at the blank white wall beside him. There was no shadow, nothing but a clean white emptiness, a curious quiet that infected the edges of his own happy mixture of noises.

Sal left his seat and peeked round from his cubicle. Megan had not arrived. All her machines sat lifeless and grey, her files all laid out ready, all still closed.

Sal glanced around the office.

There were his colleagues, each getting on with their day in their own little cells, their small shadows squirming behind the soft white walls. There were his supervisors, gaudy figures in executive business attire, stalking slowly down the aisles, gripping clipboards, peering into cubicles, making notes.

Sal turned about. A supervisor was standing just behind him. A tall man with a narrow bony face and fine blue eyes. He stooped as he looked down at the larval. He smiled kindly. He could see Sal was not in his place. He stood watching, waiting to see what the larval would do.

Sal stepped smartly into Megan's cell. He considered the arrangement of files, tapping his fingers on the table thoughtfully, before taking the nearest folder. He held it up, he considered it some more, then moved back past the supervisor without a glance and seated himself once again at his own low desk.

And the tall man smiled, and nodded, and made a mark on his board, and peered into Megan's cold empty cubicle, and made another mark, and moved on.

•

It was nearing midday. Megan had still not made an appearance.

Sal's mind was only partly on his work. He was forever listening for some slight shuffle of noise that might be her.

He worried that this was all his doing, that there had been something important she'd said, something he himself had missed. He tried carefully to think back. He tried to imagine the possibilities. But he lacked the ability to imagine very deeply. All he could picture was

Megan at work in her cell or Megan's cell empty. There was nothing else.

Sal looked at his neatly organised and ordered stack of printouts. He searched for the most sensitive of his files, its importance denoted by a fine red-and-white striped band. Sal took it and headed off down the corridors, and down the stairs, and into the archives, searching for the file's allotted place.

His hands shook as they worked the turners on the filing cabinets. This was not his job. He feared at any moment he'd be found out. But no one questioned him. No one stopped him.

It was only when he dropped into the pay-room next door that the three larvals at work inside looked up from their counting mats and stared at him with black unblinking eyes.

Sal swallowed. He tried to explain.

'I wasn't sure. About when I arrived today. Just need to check. To be sure. For me. For my own records. I didn't mark it. I like to. I always write it down. So I know.'

He edged over to the relevant books.

'Just for myself. I can do it. I'll check. It won't take long. It's just here. I just need to be certain.'

The other larvals ignored him, their eyes turning back to their work.

Sal found his entry for the day, its timing neatly marked off. He looked for Megan's. His fingers quivered. His whole body pulsed. He hunched himself around the entry book, protecting it. He had a pen ready in his pocket, ready to fill in Megan's gap for her.

There was no need. Sal stopped shaking. Beside Megan's name the box was already filled.

PERMITTED ABSENCE

Sal stood up straight. He blinked. He closed the book and shoved it back on the shelf.

'That's all now. Thank you. I've checked it. It's done. It's as it is. As it should be.'

Hurriedly he left the room.

Only one of the pay-room larvals looked up this time, watching as Sal scuttled off. Once he was gone they glanced towards the book that had been taken from the shelf. They rose and went to it. They stared at it for a moment. Then they reached up a blue-grey hand and slotted the book more neatly into its space.

•

At lunch Sal went out alone, and ate alone, and wandered the same routes through the shopping centre as he would have had he not been alone.

He quickened his pace past the clothes shop from which he'd stolen, turning his face away in case the attendant was at that exact moment gazing out the window. He felt hurt that Megan hadn't trusted him, that she'd made such a fuss over nothing, that she'd risked punishment, and with that his punishment too.

Sal stopped. At least nothing had yet come of Megan's actions. He doubled back. Calmly he made his way to the shop.

He would tell the truth. The fabric had intrigued him.

It had folded so small. He had not intended to take it. He didn't want it. Didn't need it. But it had fitted so neatly in the small soft dimple of his hand. It had been so easy. It was that ease more than anything that had made him do it.

Sal cupped his hands around his eyes and peered through the window to check it was the same attendant before going in. He didn't want to have to explain himself to anyone else.

Through the glass the shop itself looked dim, colourless, almost empty. Sal could see no movement, no sign of a shopkeeper lurking in the gloom. He shifted to look down another line of shelves where there seemed to be more light. There was a doorway in the opposite wall. It led off from the back of the shop.

Sal squinted, his small black eyes struggling to resolve the details. A short corridor. A brightly lit room. Two figures facing each other over a table.

And there was the attendant, with her thick red hair and her easy poise, slouching forward over the tabletop. Opposite her sat Megan. And yet it was Megan who was animated. She looked to be the one doing all the talking. The shopkeeper just sat, watching the larval, listening.

Sal pulled his face sharply back from the glass, suddenly scared that if he could see them then with a mere turn of the head they'd see him too.

He hurried away.

So Megan really was being punished. The theft had had its repercussions after all. Clearly Megan had been forced to work some hours in the shop. All unpaid. No doubt some sort of backroom drudgery work. This was her break, but even then she'd not been allowed to relax. She was having to account for herself, for her thievery, over and over.

And it was all lies. She was taking all the blame upon herself. Sal knew this to be true, else he'd be the one in there.

He examined his options carefully.

He would say nothing. When he saw Megan again Sal wouldn't mention any of it. Megan hadn't told him, so he mustn't know. That aspect was clear enough.

Back at his desk he considered how Megan would have to supply some reason for her absence when at length she returned. And Sal would believe anything she told him. He would show confusion, then concern, then understanding. He planned out his whole response. He practiced it while he worked. He perfected all the expressions he would go through.

Sal didn't mark the actual moment that Megan came back. She made no special announcement. She didn't make a sound. Sal just found himself suddenly noticing the normality of that faint shadow-shape in the cell beside his. Megan might well have been there working quietly for an hour or more.

Sal waited before acting on this change. He waited for a reason to present itself. Then he recalled the file he'd taken from Megan's cubicle. He hadn't yet opened it. He hadn't even seen what it was. He took it back now.

'This isn't mine.'

Sal stood with the file thrust out at arm's length.

Megan unbowed herself from her work. She glanced up at Sal. She glanced down at the file in his hand.

'I was in here. At the start of the day. There was a supervisor. He was behind me. I had to think. I had to do something.'

Megan didn't move. She didn't take the file. She continued looking at Sal, patiently, expectantly.

'So I took it. To seem like I'd a reason to be here. I don't know what's in it. I didn't look.'

Sal inched the file still more firmly forward.

Megan took it from him.

'Thanks. I don't mind. I'd do the same.' She placed it lazily on the very same spot from which Sal had taken it. 'And did the supervisor say anything?'

Sal hesitated a moment, straining to think of what he had practiced, and whether Megan's current reactions fitted in with anything he had anticipated or whether this question related to the file itself. But he couldn't make the thought-shapes fit. He shook his head.

'Oh, okay. That's good.' Megan turned back to her work. 'No harm done then.'

And Sal, duly dismissed, returned to his cell.

He didn't see Megan again till the end of the day. He should have felt calm with her working again beside him. All should have been normal. But Sal still felt distinctly ill at ease. And when the day's end came and he readied himself to leave, so he stood in the narrow gap to Megan's cell and saw her still bowed over her desk, working no faster or slower than before, nor making any sign that she was finishing up.

Here now Sal understood. It was all very simple. There was nothing to worry about. Megan had merely had the morning off in order to carry out her new shop duties. And now she was making up the lost hours. It had been arranged. It was accepted. He needn't discuss it with her. It was just work.

So Sal didn't say anything. He didn't want to make it awkward for her. He didn't even want to say he was going home, nor suggest he could wait if she wanted him to. Any slight question might raise the subject of her earlier absence. And surely Megan was doing a good thing. Surely she was doing this all to protect Sal, to be punished instead of him. So, very quietly, very carefully, Sal withdrew. And Megan did not turn round to watch him go.

8. Theories

Megan wasn't late on the following mornings. She arrived at the same time, and entered the building in the same long stream of office folk, and took up her appointed position in just the same manner as everyone else. She took to her work with the same sense of duty as ever she had before. She helped Sal with his own duties, just as he in turn helped out with hers.

Sal never raised the subject of his stealing or of Megan's curious behaviour afterwards. If she had a wish to raise it herself, that was up to her.

She didn't. Their lunches were the same as ever. They even passed by the same small clothes shop. And there was no hesitation or quickening of pace or glancing inside, or else of noticeably glancing away. It was as though the event had never happened, as though they had never been in such a shop.

Sal admired her for this, for her ability to let everything return to normal, without any blame being laid.

Till Megan began staying late after work; and not just on odd occasions, she was doing it every day.

There was no explanation. As before Sal did not openly question it, nor offer to stay on late along with her. And Megan in turn acted as though all was still perfectly normal, as though these were nothing more than her regular working hours.

But it wasn't normal and Sal did question it, at least

to himself. He questioned it as he travelled home each night alone, and as he lay in his room, and as he saw Megan again the next morning, acting as though all was well.

Sal theorised that if this was a further part of the punishment then the office must also know. The shop would have told Megan's workplace, naturally. It was procedure. It was to be expected. And it was for this reason that Megan was making no fuss. She was accepting anything that might happen because of it. She was acting just exactly as she should, despite none of it being her own fault.

Sal lay awake staring at the ceiling. He wondered just how far this honesty might extend, or at least Megan's perception of honesty, of having done the right thing; whether she said it had been herself or whether she said it had been Sal and yet asked to take the blame. Maybe she'd suggested he put her up to it. Though none of this seemed to fit. And if Megan had indeed told the truth then the office would know that Sal was a thief and that would surely be marked down against him. Or if Megan hadn't in fact said anything then perhaps it was simply Sal's duty to share some of the blame. Perhaps she expected it of him. Perhaps she was waiting.

But Sal couldn't be sure. There was a small gap in his understanding. A gap that he couldn't fill no matter how much strained thinking he allowed himself to practice. It was like having two bared ends of tough elastic in his mind, one the cause of all this and one the aftermath, but though he tugged and yanked at them he couldn't bring those two ends together. He just hadn't the strength of mind to tie them up.

So he formulated a plan. And one evening, having finished his allotted hours, he loitered outside the building, at a distance, behind some bushes. He didn't know when Megan might finish and he couldn't ask so he simply waited. And the sky went dark, and the city around him grew quiet, and Sal began to feel cold and stiff as he crouched, very still, across from the office block. But, nonetheless, he waited, with his small black eyes fixed upon the low wide slit of the building's entrance.

Perhaps Megan could have gone out another way. Perhaps he had already missed her, having shut his eyes without noticing, at the very moment she exited. He would wait till the building was closed. That seemed reasonable. Then at least he'd be sure.

•

When Megan came out at last she was alone.

Sal's plan was foolproof. He was certain this time that Megan could neither ignore the issue of her working more hours nor avoid accounting for her strange behaviour. Sal would not even need to question her specifically. Megan would offer the information of her own accord. She would walk right past where he was loitering on her usual way home. She would see him. He would tell her that he knew what she was doing. He would tell her that he only wished to help. That it was only fair he shared in her extra work, just as they often shared their office duties. She wouldn't be angry. She couldn't be angry. She hadn't been angry so far. It would all work out perfectly.

Except, on leaving the building, Megan, now muffled in hat and scarf, with her head down, fishing around in her shoulder bag, walked off in the wrong direction. She made off decisively, down a road that in no way would bring her to her home.

Sal started after her as soon as she was out of sight, trying to hold himself at a discreet distance. It was easy to follow her. Sal had no particular technique. If Megan did turn round and see him then that would be that. No problem. She would see him, and all would be well, and he could explain. He could pick up his plan from where he'd left off.

But Megan didn't turn, and as they both progressed deeper into a part of town Sal didn't know, and that he didn't know that Megan knew, he began to be concerned that his following her would not perhaps be something she'd look kindly on. So Sal began to wish that Megan would never turn round. He put his hood up, zipping the coat right up to the collar, the fake-fur rim of the hood making a narrow hollow into which Sal was sure Megan could not see if against all odds she did now glance behind her.

This slow and uneventful following only became difficult when Megan reached an old dirty block of flats and with a sudden sideways step turned in through the main glass entrance, the door of which no longer slid shut of its own. Here Sal had to run and peek through the glass after her. He saw Megan walk on past the lifts and begin to ascend the stairway at the end of the hall. Sal waited a moment then slipped between the doors, following at a rush.

Megan did not hide her footfalls on the stair. Sal ascended slowly behind her, a couple of flights below, keeping his back to the wall so Megan wouldn't see him if she looked down over the banisters. He had to guess which floor she turned off at by listening to the change of her footsteps. It wasn't too hard, she was making no effort to walk as softly as he was. He peeked round and into the dull brown light of the hallway and saw Megan at one end, in front of a door, key in hand. Then the doorway opened. A flicker of light fell upon Megan as she stepped inside. The door was shut behind her.

Sal zeroed in on the door's position and snuck quickly along the hall to make sure he would remember which one it had been. He could still hear Megan inside, shuffling about. He could see where her shadow interrupted the thin seam of light at the base of the door.

Sal thought to knock. He could do so. He could simply lift his hand and knock. He tried hard this time not to think of all the things that might happen if he did, of how he would explain himself, of how Megan would react. Unless she already knew. Unless she had somehow seen him following. Unless this was all part of her scheme. Perhaps even part of some elaborate joke.

Sal raised his hand, hesitated, then lowered it to the door handle. He gripped the metal tightly.

There was a burst of noise from behind the door. It so shocked Sal that he flinched and drew back to the other side of the hallway. A radio had been turned on, or perhaps a television, it didn't matter which, it was the loudness that startled him. The thin door did little to dampen the sound. Sal expected at any moment that other inhabitants on the same floor would come out and complain. He could deal with questions from Megan about his presence but not from strangers.

Sal marked the number of Megan's door and repeated it over and over in his head as he crept back down the hall to the main stairwell. He noted as he went that there was only light to be seen under one of the doors on the opposite side as he passed by. He noticed also that this fine sliver of light was similarly broken by shadow, and that the shadow wasn't moving. It was enough to make Sal more anxious, enough to expect the door might open wide at any moment.

He didn't linger.

Inspector Augustine's office was in an old red-brick building. The building was tall and narrow as though being squeezed by the two large company houses that butted up against it, and that only through the seniority of age was its presence endured at all.

Sal had hurried straight over after his own workday had ended. A few tired employees were still issuing from the mirrored glass frontages of the buildings either side. Teams of cleaners were already beginning their shifts.

The inspector's building still had its simple blue-painted door open and its fine line of window-lights on, all the way up to the roof. Inside, however, it was quiet. The receptionist glanced up briefly at Sal as he entered. She was a larval like himself, though old like Madox. It was easy to tell: her blue-grey skin had a taut polished sheen and her small black eyes were more prominent in their soft-rimmed sockets.

Sal readied himself to explain his visit as he made his way to her desk. He needed to sound decisive. He needed to sound important. He needed to adopt a tone of easy familiarity.

'Mr Augustine. I'm here to see now. I know him. He's always saying. He said I should. He told me. He said. And if I ever wanted. Then I could.'

With a practiced flick the old larval spun the registration book round on the desk and slid it forward.

Sal looked for a pen. The lady was holding one out for him. Sal looked at the column of boxes he had to fill. He studied them, pausing at one that asked for his number plate.

'But I don't own a car.'

'It doesn't matter. Just your name will do.'

'What about my address? How much of it—'

'It's fine. Just your name.'

'I do know my address. I only meant I—'

'Name is enough.'

Sal filled in his address anyway. And his full name. And everything else he felt was applicable. He wanted to do it properly. It felt important. It might in itself be some sort of test. He adopted an air of confidence as he wrote.

The old larval wasn't watching. She was readying a visitor pass. She turned the register back to herself before the boy had finished checking through his details. She scanned the entries. She paused. She looked up.

'Salvador?'

Sal stared back at her.

'You're called Salvador?'

Another test perhaps. Sal took a deep breath. He gave a short nod.

The old larval smiled blackly and turned her attention back to the pass.

'I'll just put Sal.'

The boy made no reaction, merely watched as the paper slip was tucked unevenly into its scratched plastic cover and given over to him. He chose not to say thank you. He was the visitor, the guest. He needed to be serious. He carefully clipped the pass to his coat as he walked away towards the stairs.

'You know where his office is?'

Sal paused. He didn't know exactly. Only the floor number. But the building wasn't so big. He nodded.

The stairs were narrow and steeply set. There was another old larval working at their foot with a bucket and brush. As Sal went to hold the bright blue banister he felt the workman catch hold of his sleeve and pull him back. It was an aggressive action. There'd been no warning. Sal tensed. This was the moment. This is when he'd be found out, or questioned, or made to fill in a much longer form. This is when he would swear that Mr Augustine really did know him, even that they were, in some way, friends. He held his breath and stared defiantly at the worker. But the old larval simply pointed with the end of his brush; the brush that had bright blue paint dripping from its bristles, the very same colour and glossiness as that which coated the banister. The man smiled and released him. Sal pressed himself against the wall on the other side of the stair and slid his way awkwardly upwards.

The office itself was not hard to find. Sal methodically checked the nameplates on each and every door as he passed, all the while pretending he wasn't checking. Nobody noticed or stopped him.

He knocked on Mr Augustine's door and, at a vague noise from within, entered.

Inside, the room smelt strange. It smelt like the inspector's car, but with other even less pleasant odours underneath. There was a mustiness mixed with an acrid chemical scent; of weak disinfectant, perhaps, or something else that Sal associated with the inspector, though he couldn't think what. Certainly it wasn't the paper files that lay unevenly stacked upon the desk. Sal knew all the different smells that came from paper. But there were several large plastic containers on low shelves behind the desk, and even though each was covered Sal considered the smell was probably coming from those.

The inspector was just now replacing the lid on one such container. Something thick and gloopy sloshed around inside as it was slid back deeper onto its shelf. Something dark bumped up against the misty plastic sides.

When at length Augustine turned round he appeared as cool and calm as ever. He gave no indication of surprise to see Sal in his office. He smiled benevolently, expectantly, ready to help the young larval in whatever way he was able.

•

Sal and Megan were walking from the offices late after work hours; after Megan's hours.

She'd found Sal waiting. He hadn't explained his sudden appearance, he'd simply asked her to come with him and she'd agreed. Sal led the way. It wasn't homeward, nor was it the direction in which he'd followed her the other day.

Megan felt uncomfortable. She felt irritable. She felt

heavy. She was wrapped up even more thickly than usual and she struggled to keep up with Sal's brisk pace.

'I don't want to be out for long, Sal. Are we going far?'

'I need to show you this. You need to see.'

'This being?'

'I can't tell you. Not yet. You'll see. We're meeting someone.'

Megan stopped asking. She was unfamiliar with these streets. She didn't like the thought of getting lost in them. Sal seemed at ease, despite his urgency of pace, but Megan kept looking down other roads as they passed them, roads she might otherwise have taken to get home, roads she might still take.

Sal tried to reassure her.

'It's all arranged. It's good. It won't be the best example. Not so fresh. But you'll see. He'll meet us there.'

Megan followed obediently.

'So, you don't mind that I've been on different shifts? Later shifts? This isn't about that?'

There was no response.

'Because we haven't discussed it. And I've been waiting for you to say something. I expected it. You know, at least something. Because you must have noticed.'

Sal remained silent. He concentrated on his own hurrying feet. As though they might themselves pass as his answer. He didn't like being late.

'And then there was the time I didn't come in in the morning? You remember that? Because you didn't say anything then either. And I did think—'

'It doesn't matter.'

'Because you remember that shop we went in? The one you took something from?'

'It's not necessary.'

'Because she didn't mind. You know? She was very nice about it. Like she understood, or something. And I didn't want you to be worried. So I—'

Sal stopped. He turned to face Megan, and she, almost bumping into him, stopped too. She opened her mouth to go on but Sal interrupted.

'We need to wait here.'

They seemed to be nowhere in particular. It was just another residential district. The usual big flat-faced properties. Some with lights. Some with broken windows. There was noise in one of the buildings opposite. Some sort of loud activity within, more than simply living. A party perhaps. Megan eyed the lower windows suspiciously.

'Right here? At the kerb? I mean, does it have to be here exactly?'

Sal looked about them, checking what he could see of the numbers above doors and the street signs high on the walls. Megan glanced further down the road, to where it was quieter.

'Can't we wait, you know, a little way along? Perhaps at a bus stop? Somewhere that might look as though we had an actual reason to loiter.'

Sal checked on a bit of paper he took from his pocket.

'No. Here. He won't be long. He said he wouldn't be long.'

So they waited.

And the noise opposite continued. It might have been music, but it was mixed with so much other noise that whatever music it might have been was obviously of little importance. And there were dull thuds, and the squeaking of doors. And Megan stared and looked away and looked again and hoped that the outside door would not itself open. And Megan decided that talking would be a better way to be discovered if anyone did indeed come through that door.

'Because if you don't mind me not telling you then that's fine. Because it must mean you trust me. That's what I think. Just as I trust you. In that you're not telling me what we're doing here.'

'I can't. I don't want to. Not yet. Not till he arrives.'

'Yes. I get that. And you see how I'm not even asking who *he* is? Because I trust you. It's a bit like a secret, you see?'

'It's not a secret.'

'Yes. Maybe. Not this. Not for you. But it's *like* one. And I respect secrets. Because if you don't want to tell me something then you must have your reasons. And perhaps it isn't even your own secret. That makes even more sense, I think. Maybe it's the secret of this mystery friend we're meeting.'

'He's not a mystery. I've talked about him before.'

Megan considered this, briefly, then dismissed it.

'But if it *was*, and if *he* was, and if the secret was *his*, then of course you couldn't say, because then it wouldn't be your secret to share. And similarly if I—'

The door opposite opened and two figures emerged,

the noise behind them enlarging temporarily then dulling once more as the door banged shut. The two figures did not walk away but stood on the pavement just outside, talking quietly. They were tall and shabbily dressed. Both were clearly larval, though neither of respectable working stock.

Megan thought it better to continue with her chatter rather than stare.

'Because if I was holding a secret, for example. I mean someone *else's* secret, not my own. Then of course I couldn't share it with you. No matter how long I've known you. Because there are some things—'

'Hey!'

The call had come from across the street.

'Because some things need to stay hidden, exactly *because* of what they are. And it's because I do trust you, because I respect you, and also for your own safety, sort of. Well, at least in a—'

'Hey, you can come over if you like! You don't need to wait outside. Real cold outside. Come on over!'

Megan waved politely but dismissively.

'Because it wouldn't really be my choice not to share something. And it's not because a secret couldn't be trusted with you. But then if it's not my secret, not wholly, not exactly, if you see what—'

'We won't harm you. We're the same. And it's so much warmer in. And there's food! You can have some. Plenty to spare. We're just like you. Maybe a little less chubby, but still—'

The other figure laughed.

'It's alright. Thank you.' Again Megan waved in what she hoped was a friendly manner; in what she hoped was a firm suggestion that she would not be coming over the road and that she did not want them crossing over either. 'We're meeting someone. He'll be here very soon.'

The figure doing the talking stepped to the kerb and looked both ways down the empty silent road, then back towards the two young larvals.

'Very soon, you say? Does this person walk like real quick?'

'He drives.'

It was Sal who provided this apparently crucial piece of information. He spoke it matter-of-factly, as though it was nothing, but it seemed to satisfy the strangers opposite. They nodded and smiled and went back inside.

Megan stared at the closed door for a moment. Then vaguely, dreamily, she turned to Sal.

'Do I—do I really look *chubby*?'

Megan knew the comment had been directed at her specifically and it scared her.

Sal said nothing.

'Could he really see that from across the street? Even with all I've got on? Do—do you see it? Sal?'

Sal checked the bit of paper again. He checked the street name, the building number. He checked the hour he'd noted down.

'He'll be here soon.'

Megan breathed deeply and then began strolling away. Sal became agitated, though he made no move to follow her.

'Wait. No. You mustn't. We need to wait. He said he'll be here. We must—'

'I understand, Sal. But he's not here. And I don't like standing around on strange roads.'

She was walking back the way they had come, her head bowed.

Sal started after her then stepped back, glancing again at the number on the door.

'You must stay. We need to wait. Just here.'

'I don't want to wait, Sal. I want to go.' Megan began walking backwards. 'Your friend is late. He may not come at all. I want to trust you, yes. But why should I trust him?'

Sal didn't have an answer.

'So, do you want to come with me? Do you want to accompany me home?' Megan gave a nervous laugh. 'And do *you* think I'm getting chubby, Sal? Have you noticed but chosen not to mention it?'

'I don't know.' Sal itched to step forward, to follow her, but returned again to his agreed waiting spot. 'I don't understand. Why he's not. I don't know. I promised. I wanted you to see something. You needed to see it. It's necessary. He promised to show you.'

'Then it can wait too. And if he's late, or not coming, then it can't be all that important, right? And I don't want to be here any more, Sal. Not at this hour. I'll see you tomorrow.'

She turned away decisively and strode back down the street.

Sal waited, hoping as he watched her go that he would

hear the sudden hum of an engine, that the inspector would arrive and they could both rush back down the road after the slowly retreating Megan.

But when at last Sal did hear a car approaching, and it was indeed Mr Augustine, and the headlights were flashed upon his seeing Sal, Megan was already long away.

Sal knew where she'd gone. He knew the route she'd be taking. But he couldn't tell the inspector. And he couldn't let Megan down by their following her.

Augustine stepped out of the car. He straightened up. He eyed Sal quizzically.

'I thought you were bringing your friend along.'

'She had to go.'

'Oh. I see.'

Augustine glanced at the building. He surveyed the street around him. He locked the car.

'Well, shall we go up anyway?'

Sal nodded obediently and followed the inspector inside.

10. A Disappearance

They didn't discuss the matter when they were next at work. Megan never enquired as to what Sal had wanted to show her, nor the identity of his friend. Sal never let on that he guessed where she'd gone to when she left him standing at the kerb.

They both kept to their work. They shared their lunch hours. They spoke about inconsequential matters like the constant recycling of printouts, or implausible inventions for making their work easier, such as pens that moved just by thinking, or self-folding paper. And Megan grew each week a little fatter. And Sal pretended he didn't see.

Till one day Megan didn't come into work.

The first day it happened Sal tried hard to ignore the matter and so said nothing. But by the third morning of Megan's absence Sal's unease had grown to less manageable levels. At his desk he got little done, partly from lack of concentration, partly because he hoped his own inactivity would not go unnoticed. When a shadow lingered at the entrance to his cubicle he turned round sharply to address the supervisor.

She was new. They changed so frequently. This one stood now with a kindly expression, her clipboard pressed to her chest beneath loosely-folded arms.

Sal addressed her at once.

'Where's Megan?'

The supervisor looked only mildly bemused. The question seemed to have an accusatory overtone.

'At her new job, I presume.'

Sal considered this. He clenched his jaw. The supervisor meanwhile peered over him to the neat stacks of printouts, seemingly untouched. She entered the cubicle and began counting the items in the out-tray. Sal ignored the activity.

'You mean here? A new job? A promotion?'

'No.' The supervisor was only half-listening. 'In a shop, or some such place. I wrote her a reference. A general letter of recommendation. Nothing particular. I'd have thought she would have told you.'

The supervisor straightened. She began making notes on her clipboard.

Sal tried to think quickly.

'We had an argument.' He didn't want to give anything away. 'I wasn't sure if she'd been successful. In her application. The job. The shop. She never said.'

But the supervisor wasn't listening, only nodding and smiling to the sound of the larval's voice as she backed out of the cubicle and walked away.

At lunch Sal headed straight to the clothes store he'd stolen from. He paused briefly before entering, looking through the glass to see who might be there, then he pushed open the door and into the soft fabric warmth of the shop's interior.

It was quiet and still inside, just as it had been the first time he'd visited. There was no attendant. The shelves had been rearranged. The colours and shapes of the clothing were all different. They glistened. Sal pretended to look. His hands instinctively crept to his pockets, but he drew them out sharply and let them hang by his sides.

He positioned himself near the inner doorway he'd seen before, the one that led to the kitchen. There was a muted hissing coming from behind it, and when it opened, and when the attendant came out, Sal tried hard to look past her. But he saw nothing.

The attendant smiled. If she recognised him at all she didn't show it.

'Is there something in particular you're after? Someone you're buying for? A new hat, perhaps?'

She made her way to the front desk and stationed herself behind it, leaning forward with her elbows on the counter. From a small plastic tube she squirted a worm of cream onto the back of her hand and massaged it into her skin, all the while staring fixedly at Sal.

The larval hesitated. He couldn't ask. Not directly. Not in the same way he'd spoken to the supervisor.

If he said anything now about Megan he might be suggesting he knew something he shouldn't, and in so doing give away something that Megan wanted to keep hidden. Then again perhaps he really did know nothing at all.

'I'm not sure. No. Yes. A hat. Perhaps.'

The attendant stood up straight. She scrunched her fingers absentmindedly into her long red hair as she glanced over at the stock. Then she squinted and looked back at Sal.

'For yourself?'

A moment of recognition, maybe. Sal stood firm.

'Yes.'

The attendant raised her eyebrows. The clothing in the shop was for women, not really for larvals. But she shrugged and led him to the appropriate section.

'I'm not sure there'll be anything your size. What colour were you thinking? There may just be—'

She began lifting out various examples but Sal interrupted quickly.

'No. I agree. They're not really. Mmm. I don't think—' Sal backed slowly away, nodding and smiling, just as he'd seen the supervisor do. 'You're right. Not for me. I just. No. I must go. I made a mistake.'

Hurriedly he left the shop.

•

It was an hour after work and fully dark when Sal reached the building to which he had once followed Megan.

It was quiet, as before, and Sal was not this time following anyone, nor trying not to be seen, but still he proceeded upwards through the building with that same slow caution, pausing even to check the echo of his own footsteps as he ascended the narrow stairwell.

When he came to Megan's door again he stopped.

On the last occasion, standing just outside it, he'd been sure that Megan had gone through. He'd seen her.

That was surety enough. But now he felt he couldn't be certain it was actually the same door.

He checked the number. It could have been changed. He might have misremembered it. He moved off again down the hallway. He came back. He listened through the door's thinness. There was that same sharp garbled hum of radio or television, not quite as loud as before, but loud enough.

In his pocket Sal carried a short rectangle of tough flexible plastic. He always carried it. Its simplicity intrigued him. He'd never actually used it, but he'd seen Mr Augustine use something similar. He'd asked how it worked then later sought out the very same type of plastic himself. It made him feel important to carry such an item. And no one could reprimand him if they found it in his possession. One surely couldn't be punished for carrying a piece of flexible plastic.

Now Sal pushed the smoothed edge carefully between the door and its thin frame, just next to the slot for the key, letting the plastic bend and slip itself round the double corner of the jamb.

There came no satisfactory click to let him know that he'd done it correctly. The door simply opened a short way inwards, away from the springy pressure of the plastic.

A narrow gap. A vertical seam of light.

Sal thought there might be a chain, so he pushed the door only gently. But there was no chain. With a long low juddery squeak the door swung open, exposing the bright room within.

The unexpected creaking panicked the larval. He feared that someone else in the building might hear, that from across the hall someone would come and discover him, his piece of plastic still in hand.

So Sal stepped on inside the room and without hesitation shut the door quickly behind him.

II. Interruptions

Sal was familiar with the smallness of such living spaces.

'…and in doing so may endeavour to create an elaborate ruse by which its brood can be concealed…'

He had seen several in the company of the inspector but they were usually in a state of disrepair, and they stank.

This one was bright and tidy. Its air was fresh. Though it was still more cramped than even Sal would have expected.

'…with the strongest of the hatchlings not necessarily being the one to survive when all other factors…'

There was a single main room, a kitchen in one corner, a mattress for a bed in another. One further door, closed, suggested a separate small bathroom.

The corner-kitchen was exceptionally clean. The surfaces were sparkling. It was either wholly unused or else used by someone particularly fastidious in their habits. It was hard to say which.

'…whereas the weakling in avoidance of confrontation may find itself at an advantage if discovered by…'

The mattress, though only a mattress and raised on a few thick lengths of wood to give it some air underneath, was nonetheless tidy, with tucked-in sheets and well-plumped pillows and blankets turned back on themselves.

'...and despite such initial abandonment are nonetheless provided for at the outset of...'

There was a wardrobe against the wall near the foot of the mattress. In front of the wardrobe, at the room's centre, was a wide couch. The couch faced a low table, and upon the table was a pocket-sized radio set.

'...where such an innate sense of abandonment can be countered by a simple willingness to forget whether or...'

The radio seemed a great deal louder now that Sal was in the apartment. Its noise was tinny and intrusive, a sharpness against which Sal was finding it hard to think.

'...having been born equal a shift in status within the group can be conferred through the application of...'

Too loud to be bearable for someone inside the room.

'...the group voice being more powerful than that of the individual, usually to the detriment of that individual when...'

The sort of loudness that suggested it was meant to be heard through doors, or even walls.

'...that the individual's default position is always to believe it knows best and that it will readily defend that position...'

Sal approached the radio and very slowly turned down its volume, all the while staring at what he presumed was the door to the bathroom.

'...evidence to the contrary, where any retreat from impending argument is itself a measure by which to further protect self-interest...'

He hoped this change in volume would prompt a response. He expected a rattle of noise, a sudden suck of water, perhaps even a vocalization of some sort. But there was nothing.

'...of such an attack against the other being at heart a defence of the fundamental idea of the self...'

The radio was plugged into the wall by way of a timer, with little green switches round the timer's dial for the radio to come on and off at certain hours throughout the day.

'...likewise acts that purport to be of benefit to others are still ultimately in the service of the self...'

Sal examined the dial. He touched his soft grey fingertips to some of the tiny green switches.

'...and the automatic preservation of the self is merely a continuance of the singular known state of the self...'

The switches were especially sensitive. Several at once flicked inward to their off-positions. Sal touched some more.

'...where that self-centredness can then be utilised to...'

The radio went silent behind him. Sal glanced sharply at the bathroom door again, waiting, straining for the slightest sound. Still nothing.

He approached the door. He put the small hole of his ear against its thinly painted surface. He knocked. He pressed down upon the handle, expecting to find it locked, but the handle turned and the door swung inwards.

The bathroom was in darkness, but by the light of the main room Sal could see it was as clean as the rest of the apartment. A narrow grey tub. Pink lagging exposed underneath. Broad grey-painted pipes protruding from the walls.

It was a cold room. Sal closed the door again.

He pulled himself tall like the inspector. He breathed in deeply, calmly, as he'd seen the inspector do. He set about examining the main room more thoroughly.

It had occurred to him that it might not be Megan's apartment at all, but he soon found evidence that reassured him he'd not just stepped into a stranger's home. There was a small cloth bag on the arm of the couch. Megan's multicoloured cap lay on top of it. Then Sal noticed her keys, with their squidgy glow-worm fob, sitting on a plate just beside the kitchen sink.

Sal's body pulsed. He looked to the main door.

'She's just gone out. She can't be long. Not without her keys. Not without her hat.'

He could still leave. He could retrace his way back down the stairs, perhaps meeting Megan coming up. Or he could wait outside, across the street, watching for her to return.

But what would be the difference if she found him waiting out there as opposed to in here? He'd have to explain his presence either way.

'I didn't know. I got worried. You hadn't been seen for days. You disappeared.'

He went to the one thin slit of a window. He peeked out between the blinds.

'I followed you here. Weeks ago. I never told anyone. It was a secret. I know. But I worried. I wanted to help.'

The view from the window was obscured to one side by a blank projecting wall. Beyond was the city's blackness, punctuated with points of light from other buildings, windows, streetlights far below. But it was the wrong direction for Sal to look in. He wouldn't see Megan returning from this angle.

'Just a bit of food shopping. Yes. I see now. That's all you needed. But I can help. I didn't mean to startle you. Let me help.'

There was a small mint-green refrigerator under the serving area, a little rusted down one of its front edges, but humming smoothly. Sal opened it. A fine mist poured out. The interior wasn't merely chilled, the machine had been set to its lowest temperature. Every spare bit of space was crammed with unopened packages. Hard cheese and cured meats predominated.

Sal stood. He checked the cupboard spaces. All the shelves were stacked with tins, boxes of dry biscuit, thin bars of cheap chocolate. None of it was Megan's usual fare.

'I understand. You felt you had to get in something fresh. Something green. Yes. Something good to suck on.'

Sal sat on the couch and stared into the middle of the room. Sal went and lay on the low bed. Sal reached for the timer and, flicking the tiny green switches, turned the radio back on.

'...*inherent to the individual and manifesting as a deep-seated inability to look beyond their own immediate needs*...'

Sal rose and continued exploring.

He checked the main door's lock to be sure he hadn't inadvertently shut it completely. He felt it had been far too easy for him to get in. He would suggest Megan at least got some sort of chain. He could help with the fittings. He would make himself as helpful as possible. As soon as he saw her again he would give her this crucial advice. That way she would know he was on her side.

'...*to a similar extent in regards group interest by also lacking the ability to see beyond their own unquestioning conformity*...'

He checked the wardrobe. It opened stiffly. It was as stuffed full with clothes as the fridge had been with food.

'...*as evidenced by the undesirous consequences of former actions will continue to act freely and even in the same manner as before when this can be perceived as*...'

The wardrobe was filled with clothes the likes of which Sal had never seen Megan wearing. Some still had small cardboard tags attached to their sleeves. These were simple, handwritten. The prices were all low.

'...*whereby this capacity for freedom of action inevitably gives rise to a sense of freedom from responsibility, which in turn*...'

And now as Sal looked more closely at the worn fabrics, the crudely patched elbows and fraying cuffs, he could see that these were not new clothes at all. They each came from a variety of secondhand shops.

'...*even more pronounced deformities can themselves be of benefit in promoting a stronger instinct for survival in any individual unfortunate enough to*...'

There was among the hanging garments a long dark-purple dress. It reached right down to the floor of the wardrobe. Its material seemed so smooth it might have been silk, though it was much thicker, heavier, glossier. Even secondhand that ought to have been expensive.

'...*where such deformations are due to insufficient nutrients having been provided before the phase being entered into*...'

Sal tried wrapping some of the fabric round his hand. It didn't burn, nor sting, nor even itch.

'...*though external environmental factors beyond the individual's awareness can also contribute to early eclosure if indeed...*'

He reached up to unhook the dress. The hanger fell away from his grip. It fell backwards into the wardrobe without a sound. It disappeared entirely, taking the purple dress with it.

'...*a latent delicacy upon emergence that requires the proper conditions in which to harden fully, aided by a protective film that soon...*'

Sal got down on his knees. Blindly he reached out his arm, groping under the other clothes to retrieve the dress. But the more he reached forward into the wardrobe the more his hand kept going.

'...*as prone to infection at this delicate stage as prior to eclosure, though better equipped to fight against it so long as...*'

Till Sal had his head and shoulders between the drapery of clothing.

'...*features within earlier development being now most prominent all further energies will be devoted to this singular aim...*'

Till Sal was on his hands and knees inside the wardrobe.

'...*all being dependant on their initial choice of concealment where early discovery may lead to the termination of...*'

Till Sal fell off the back lip of the wardrobe and landed bodily in an open space of darkness, his face now pressing into something soft and warm and damp.

12. PUPA

Shifting threads of light seeping in from tiny irregular gaps in the wardrobe's disturbed barricade provided Sal with a brief glimpse of the space he'd fallen into, before the clothes settled themselves once more and all became dark.

Sal lay still for a moment. He'd found the purple dress. He'd landed on it. The air around him was hot and damp. It was stifling. The radio came now muffled from behind him, its chatter deadened by the portal of heavy clothes.

The room was not, in fact, entirely dark. Once Sal's eyes had accustomed themselves to the dimness he thought he could just make out the faint orange square of a single window. It glowed only slightly, its panes pasted over with layers of newspaper print. The light from it was just enough for Sal to get his bearings, enough to give him a sense of being in a real room, not merely a warm wall-less expanse.

Sal stood. He groped for the wardrobe behind him. He reached through the gap to the damp-edged fabric. He felt around the doorframe bordering the hole. He touched upon the door itself, hanging loosely open. He tried pushing it closed but it only swung wide again.

Sal felt for the light-switch, found it, tried it. Nothing. He explored this new space methodically, practically, feeling at first along the nearest wall, edging his way round towards the window opposite. His hand touched upon a radiator and he drew back sharply at the sudden heat. Trying then to manoeuvre on past the radiator he stumbled against a heavy bucket. He crouched. The bucket was near full of lukewarm water.

As he went further Sal discovered several shallow trays. These were pushed close to the walls. They each had small retreating puddles within them. The walls themselves were covered in a thin film of moisture. The ceiling dripped.

Not far beyond the window was a couch. It was old and worn. It was smaller than the one in the front room. Its upholstery was torn at the arms. Its top edge felt slippery with something much thicker than water. At one end of the seat Sal discovered the figure of a naked girl. All he saw of her at first was a dim pale glow, a glow far too faint for Sal to have seen before his eyes had settled to the comparative darkness. If he looked at her directly, aspects of her form disappeared. He had to keep shifting his focus, letting his small black eyes flicker over her, trying to get a sense of her overall shape.

The girl was little more than a large huddled lump, curled in one corner, her knees brought up to her chest, her arms trapped tight beneath the soft scissor of her legs, the smooth round dome of her head bowed forward, resting on her knees.

Sal slowly seated himself at the couch's opposite end, careful not to wake the girl, gazing at her through the dark, willing her not to be Megan. Even when his eyes had adjusted as much as they were likely to, he still wasn't sure it was her. That skin was too pale, and she was fatter still than when he'd seen her last, misshapen by the sag of her own weight.

If the girl woke now, Megan or not, Sal wondered how he would explain his presence, his sudden proximity. He alone was aware of his own good intentions, how he only had her safety in mind. She might wake altogether angry, furious to be so exposed. There'd be no time to go through the details of his having discovered her like this, by accident. It was all so complicated. Unless of course she was too sleepy to understand him all at once. Then he might be able to soothe her with lengthy explanations. Then he would be able to convince her that she was much safer for him now knowing where she was, that he could protect her, if only she would allow him to, if at last she might draw him into her secret.

In that sense Sal considered it would be much better for him to wake her on purpose, gently, right away, than to allow her the shock of discovering him herself. He reached forward to touch upon her knee. Just one small touch upon her knee would surely be acceptable. She couldn't be angry about that. He'd just shake her knee a little till she stirred. But as Sal reached out, as he watched the dim shape of his hand getting nearer, as he imagined touching her, rocking her awake, he sensed that something was not at all right. There was an eerie silence about her, an uncanny stillness.

The girl hadn't moved in her sleep all the while Sal had been sitting by her, staring at her in the dark. There had been no sudden deep breath in nor long sigh out. There'd been no shifting of position, none of the usual tiny movements that one unconsciously associated with the living.

Yet neither did she seem quite unalive. There was a definite sense of vitality about her. In how her pale skin drew in the sparse particles of light and held them. In how the moisture that had collected on her skin shimmered, ever so slightly, as though moved by some fine vibration, constant yet unseen. The girl seemed to glow very faintly, fuzzily in the dark. And when Sal's outstretched fingertips did at length touch her, lightly, on her ankle, there was a distinct warmth to her skin. It wasn't merely the ambient warmth of the room given back, it came from an inner source.

There was heat beneath that skin. And the skin itself felt strange. It felt harder than it should. It felt to Sal as though, if he pushed a little more, just a little, the skin might buckle and crack, that it might split, and the Megan that was inside might then spill out.

A doll-like casing, toughened, keeping her safe within. But how thick or thin that casing might be, whether brittle like a shell or yielding like a membrane, Sal couldn't be certain. And the state of Megan underneath, whether still mostly as he'd known her, or whether she had already turned to mush, beginning that liquid phase in which she would dissolve into herself to then grow again, there was no way for Sal to be sure. The process could not be stopped once started. It couldn't be reversed. And to rupture that outer casing, even slightly, would mean her slow and silent death.

How easy it would be.

Sal withdrew his hand. Then, fearing even his presence might disturb her, he retreated carefully, softly, from the room. Lifting the damp purple dress from the floor, he pulled it back through the wardrobe with him, and closing the wardrobe's plain white door, Sal stood once again in the main room, wincing at its overbearing brightness, with the radio chattering earnestly behind him.

13. Liquids

The room was thick with the pressure of hot wet air. The darkness fizzed. It seethed. It felt like it might overflow. It felt like it might burst. The moisture that touched upon the walls had thickened still further. It had become a layer of milky gunge that slowly, gloopily, made its way down over the old plaster to spread across the floor.

A fine black split in one dark wall resolved itself into a door. As it widened there came a fine rising hiss from beyond it. A radio's crackle and whine. A noise beginning low then steadily winding up to a high thin pitch. Its energy building, before it suddenly cracked, tearing away from itself, to begin its low tone once again. And each time that hiss rose the hot wet air buzzed with raw electrical current, before it too snapped back to a low shiver, just as the charge was released.

There was a lean dark figure in the black of the open door. Despite the juddering loop from the radio he slimed his way smoothly into the room. And as he came closer so too other figures emerged. They came oozing up through holes in the floorboards. They bulged outwards then separated from the thick wet walls.

Sal lay silent in his bed. He tried to curl up small and tight, shrinking himself away from the intruders. He pulled the thin topsheet of his bedclothes over his head but still he could see the figures emerging and advancing as the radio whined and hissed and cracked and whined and hissed and cracked.

Sal tried to dissolve into the darkness. But Sal himself was not entirely dark. He was giving off a faint yellow glow. No matter how tightly he buried himself inside himself they would see him. And they did. And they came on right towards him. They whispered to each other as they came. They whispered to Sal. They beckoned.

'You can come out now. We're just like you. You're quite safe. You can show yourself in all your rounded glory. We won't do you any harm. You're just like us.'

They laughed softly. Their soft laughter blended with the radio's whine, climbing and breaking. It thickened still further the wetness of the air.

Sal tried closing his eyes, hoping to shut out his own small light, hoping to disappear. But he could still see the figures through the thin outer membrane of his eyelids. Each dark shape slowly advancing. Dim shadowy people.

'You're getting fat. You're ripening. Don't you get too big now. Don't let yourself squirm away.'

But Sal could not get away. He couldn't move. He felt very heavy. He felt his own weight holding him down. There was no strength left in the fluid of his insides. There was nothing but its uniform outward press, with him no more than a vague consciousness, adrift in a soup of himself.

The figures were all around him. They pawed soft-limbed at his fatness. They were trying to unzip him from himself. Their long black fingers groped at his tough outer skin, hoping to find an edge, a lip to prise up, from which to peel him back, to open him out.

And Sal watched from inside as those long dark fingers found that one weak spot. A small uneven flap that tore gently as they bent it back, letting in a new brightness. And along with that brightness it let in the figures themselves, as they pushed their slim shadow-shapes right inside him.

And as they filled the space that was his own private space, so Sal's own warm lightness, his own inner liquids, seeped away. A slow spread, an even dispersal as the figures entered, filling him up in emptying him out.

Till Sal sank into the torn and slimy cushions of the couch. Till there was no more of him to be drained. Till the figures themselves now lay where he had lain.

And he could feel their weight pressing down into the hot wetness of himself. And he was helpless to do anything but listen to their slow breathing, their wheezing, their moaning, above his own warm sodden existence.

A long low whine: rising, fizzing, cracking, beginning again.

•

Madox had already left for work when Sal emerged from his room. But still Sal stood on the upper landing and listened for a good while before making his way down the narrow stair and into the dim daylight of the kitchen.

In his arms he carried a bundle of loosely balled-up sheets. He listened again, to be sure Madox was not in fact hiding elsewhere in the house, then stuffed the sheets down through the wide round hole of their washing machine, added a generous cup of milky detergent, and turned the dial for a boil wash.

Up once more in his foul-aired room Sal gathered and counted out several fresh sets of clothing. These he ordered and layered into a large canvas bag. On top of this he laid a fresh packet of the mild grey soap he insisted upon, plus the rasp he used on his gums. He didn't need anything else.

Sal stood the stripped mattress on its edge against the wall to dry, opening the bedroom window a crack to mix out the smell. Shouldering his packed bag he returned downstairs to the rumble of the machine, wrote a short note for Madox and left it on the kitchen table, weighted with an empty glass.

From his coat pocket he took his set of housekeys and, adding to it one key more, complete with squidgy rubber glow-worm fob, he stepped out of the house.

The locks Sal purchased were of the cheaper sort. There were some much stronger, more expensive brands of lock that he'd eyed, and felt the weight of, and imagined the resilience of, but those had complicated fittings; the cost of them required the additional cost of professional tools and an expertise in home improvement that Sal felt he did not yet possess.

He returned to Megan's apartment with several simple chain-locks instead, as well as a bag of thin black nails, a single screwdriver and a claw hammer.

He put the radio on.

'...during this season the monotreme will seek out a vacant burrow and take up residence, with the beetle arriving soon after once the monotreme's presence has been asserted...'

Sal made a short sweep of the apartment, checking everything was in place, just as he had left it. With a small pocket torch he peeked through to the back room to ensure all was well, letting its fine beam fall upon the pale unmoving figure.

Retreating again he quietly closed up the wardrobe and set to work on the apartment's main door.

'...though the monotreme only uses the burrow for sleeping, venturing far out each day for food, the beetle is far more likely to stay inside at all hours...'

Each yellow-metal lock came with its own plastic-pouched set of screws. But the problem was as Sal had anticipated, he couldn't get the screws to bite into the wood of either the door or the jamb without having first drilled a neat hole to guide in the thread, and he owned no drill. Instead he gently tapped in a nail on each spot he'd marked out for the screws.

'...*the beetle, in being unpalatable to the monotreme and as such of no immediate threat, will be allowed to share the same space without concern or even notice...*'

Sal had intended to pull the first nail back out when he thought it had gone in deep enough. In so doing it would provide the hole down which a screw could follow. But the nail held fast, and the fitting for the lock seemed secure enough with only these black nails holding it in place.

'...*the beetle's fastidious nature ensures a constant cleanliness within the burrow, without any such upkeep provided by the monotreme...*'

Sal fixed up four of the locks, from the very top of the door right down to the bottom. It took him longer than expected, an extra gentleness being required when hammering; the fine metal shafts of the nails often had sharp protrusions along their short lengths and Sal had no wish to let them catch upon his papery skin.

'...*the two have little interaction with each other during their cohabitation, as though ignoring or else wholly unaware of each other's presence...*'

Neither did Sal wish to make too much noise in his work, it might attract unwanted attention elsewhere in the building. As such he would stop, every once in a while, and listen for noises out in the hallway. He even smeared the door's hinges with cooking oil in hope of eradicating the squeak, with only limited success.

'...*in partial payment for its chores the beetle extracts essential nutrients from faeces left by the monotreme, any indigestible parts being duly removed from the burrow*...'

With all the locks in place, and all the chains looped across, Sal tested them. He opened the door slowly, waiting for each of the chains to pull taut. But his measurements had been off. To begin with only the top chain caught, the others stayed comparatively slack.

Sal didn't mind. If the door was forced further the other locks would catch. Or if one chain failed then the others might hold. It would at least give Sal time to react to any potential intruder.

'...*most of the beetle's day is taken up with this work, having built itself a much smaller nest in a corner of the burrow inaccessible to the much larger monotreme*...'

Sal stood looking at his work, his new hammer in hand, feeling the weight of it, imagining its blunt head coming down on any fingers that tried to push in and around the frame of the door.

'...*by its presence alone the monotreme acts as a deterrent to other would-be predators, ensuring relative safety for the housekeeper-beetle*...'

Sal had two locks left. He fitted one in the bathroom. It wasn't necessary but it enabled him to test his idea of removing the nails and adding screws. It worked well enough.

'...*with the monotreme having laid several leathery white eggs the beetle makes itself scarce, its forced removal from the* burrow during this period becoming a natural instinct for the monotreme…'

The bathroom lock was now much stronger than those on the front door. Sal considered removing the nails in order to start again. He tried with one of the locks but its nails were hammered in far too deep.

'…such eggs if found unprotected will not be considered by the beetle as diverse from any other foodstuffs previously secreted by the monotreme…'

Sal opened the front door again, checking how far it would go, estimating how easily a hand might be pushed inside. As he glanced through the gap he saw movement. There was someone in the hallway, one of the building's other residents: an old female larval. She stood sidelong in the dim corridor, as though she too had stopped to listen. Now, at the sound of the chains, she turned and stared at Sal through the narrow gap in the doorway, her small black eyes fixed on his.

'…the eggs, although too large to be transported, will none-theless be punctured one by one in the beetle's own unsuccessful efforts to move them…'

The old larval had an inquisitive look. She turned bodily to come closer. Sal shut the door.

He waited.

After a short while he heard the larval's footsteps retreating slowly down the hall.

'…on finding the broken eggs the monotreme will be unaware of the beetle's interference and will simply vacate the burrow, with the beetle's own exit effected soon after…'

Sal turned the radio off. He needed to keep an ear out.

He set to work securing the last of the locks, placing it on the inner door that extended behind the wardrobe. The door was not meant to shut completely. The chain merely ensured it would not keep hanging wide open and that any curious hands groping through the muddle of clothes would find a hard unyielding surface rather than a gaping hole.

Sal sat to have his lunch. He ate slowly and methodically, chewing each mouthful to a fine pulp as he stared at the opposite wall. He cleared away after himself, leaving everything spotless, then set about replenishing the water trays in the back room.

Sal went over Megan with a damp cloth. He worked gently. He listened to her. He put his earhole to different places upon her hardened skin. He thought he could hear a dim wash of noise, sometimes the faintest of gurgles, but he couldn't be sure over whether such sounds came from inside Megan or himself.

Sal wiped down the walls lest a mould should develop, returning the gooey moisture to the buckets. Then he refreshed the buckets also, and checked the corners of the room for further deposits of slime. He worked by torchlight, ever careful over where he pointed the beam, not wishing to dazzle the sleeping doll-like figure. The light-fitting in the ceiling of that room hung empty. Perhaps it had been one of Megan's initial preparations, though Sal never located the missing bulb.

Having arranged everything in the apartment back to how he'd found it, Sal finally took his leave. Standing outside in the hallway, key in hand, it was only now he realised how all his improvements to the main door were of no use without someone being on the inside to secure the chains in place.

Sal went back in. He removed some of the litter of his meal from the bin and spread it about. He dirtied a few clean plates and left them on the kitchen counter. He messed up the bedding on the mattress. He wet a new bar of soap in the bathroom. He put the radio on, but quietly. Then, again, he departed. It wasn't much of a deception but it would have to do.

On his second attempt at leaving Sal noticed once more that he was not alone. The same old larval was watching him. This time she stood at the opposite end of the hallway, as though she'd been waiting all that time for Sal to make his exit. She smiled at him. She nodded encouragingly.

Sal half-lifted his hand in vague acknowledgement, then, fearing an impending conversation, he thrust the hand into the pocket of his coat and turned about. Without looking back he hurried along to the stairwell and down out of sight.

15. Not Alone

When Sal finished his workday he headed straight for Megan's apartment, though by now he'd begun to think of the place as just as much his own.

Despite his daily worries he didn't allow himself to rush. There was no rush. Either everything would be just as it should be, or it wouldn't. Being a few out-of-breath minutes early couldn't change that, and being seen going anywhere faster than was necessary might raise suspicions.

Yet nobody saw him on that particular street, entering that particular building, standing outside that particular door with his key ready-gripped in his hand. Here he paused, briefly, examining the lock in the dim brown light of the hall. There were fine scratches around the keyhole. Scratches that may or may not have been there before.

Sal listened. He could hear the usual muffled chatter of the radio. Did it seem a little louder than he'd left it? He couldn't tell. Or was it not quite loud enough? Was its deterrent now too weak to be in any way effective? He didn't know that either.

But the key slipped in easily and the lock turned and the door swung smoothly back. The lights went on at his simple touch of the switch to reveal how all was just as he'd left it, all his carefully arranged mess. So the radio had indeed done its job. Or else no one had come to the door at all that day and the radio had gone unheard. He switched it off.

Having carefully fixed the four chains in place Sal turned about once more to face the room. He put his hands on his hips. He breathed out. It all felt so easy, so commonplace. It even felt homely. He began at once to tidy up.

It didn't take long for everything to be put back in order, undoing his ruse of lived-in slovenliness. He checked the wardrobe, reaching through and pushing gently at the door beyond that served as the wardrobe's false back, feeling the tension in the chain. But he didn't go through to the space in which Megan lay curled, not just yet.

Sal shuffled back into the front room. He pottered about. He examined an ornament he hadn't noticed before, a cloudy yellow soap-stone carving of a small fat naked woman with overtly rounded features and a vacant wide-eyed expression. Sal weighed it in his hand, wondering if the object held any significance, or whether this was merely another part of the overall set-up.

'Just for show. Like everything else. Nothing of it meaning anything.'

He put the figurine back. He made himself a simple dinner, munching slowly on wilted leaves while he went on with his easy exploration.

In the bathroom he found a drawer containing several small tins of make-up, an assortment of free samples; none of them meant for larvals, all being of the wrong colour.

Sal tried some, testing a thick smear of milky brown on his own pale blue-grey cheek. He waited to see if it stung. But stinging wasn't the issue, it felt more as though he'd missed his mouth while eating. It felt greasy. Instinctively Sal had the urge to wipe it away. For such a small smear it felt strangely heavy, pulling against the soft membrane of his skin.

Sal examined himself in the mirror. It looked like he'd had an accident with a paint brush, nothing more. He smudged the waxy substance further with his fingertip. He spread it all over his cheek, then beyond. One tiny pea-sized dollop seemed to go a long way, so long as he spread it out thinly, and there was plenty of it still in the sample pot.

'She won't mind. She won't know. She won't need it.'

Sal covered his whole face with the make-up, right up and over the smooth dome of his head then down around his neck, methodically working the colour into every corner and crease, making faces to pull the skin taut, tightly closing his small black eyes so he could do around the rim of each socket and then gently over the lids.

When it was finished Sal was sure he'd done something wrong, applied the make-up incorrectly somehow. It didn't look right. Not right at all. He squinted at the mirror and waggled his head, trying to see things differently, to see in the reflection someone other than himself. But those little bead-black eyes were always there, staring back out of that strange brown face. And the brown was just one brown, all over. There was no shading, no sense of definition. It looked unnatural, nothing more than a very fine mask, and him no different beneath. It would deceive no one.

'Can't fool them. Won't fool anyone. Doesn't fool me.'

Sal being a common hairless larval didn't help matters, so he went to the wardrobe and rifled through it. He found an old cloth cap. He found a worn cotton scarf. He searched for dark glasses but there were none. He went back to the mirror. He squinted again, turning his head, trying to catch himself side on, unawares. And, for a tiny moment, just when he was tiring of the game, just when his mind was starting to drift to other matters, such as how to get the layer of make-up off, Sal thought he saw something. For a moment he'd felt there was indeed someone else in the mirror beside himself, someone else in the room.

Sal stopped. He felt uneasy. But in looking once more, merely by thinking upon it, the illusion was broken.

Sal yawned. It spoiled everything. His black gums gleamed within the dark round hole of his mouth, rimmed now by those formless wax-brown lips.

Sal washed his face and hands, thoroughly. The clothes were put away.

•

When night came Sal couldn't sleep.

The simple mattress-bed was comfortable enough. The covers were warm and didn't admit any draughts. But there were unfamiliar noises all around him, each one invading a space that Sal hadn't yet settled into. He hadn't learned how.

The larval lay with his small black eyes wide open. He listened through the darkness.

There was a thumping.

Sal sat up.

It sounded as though it came from the set of apartments directly above him. It wasn't just the sound of feet moving about, it was slow and deliberate.

Then there came a bang, much sharper and louder than the thump. Sal winced bodily. The bang had been close, on the same floor as him, out in the stairwell perhaps. There followed a short shout. Sal couldn't make out the word exactly. Maybe it wasn't even a word. It echoed, obscuring the muffle of itself still further.

Next was a scream.

Sal didn't move, even to breath, the air hanging stilled in his now open mouth.

Perhaps it hadn't really been a scream. Just something high-pitched. A squeaking of rubber soles on a tiled floor, maybe.

Laughing followed. More thumps. Another bang. Then the clear sound of booted feet running down a hallway. Perhaps Sal's own hallway. He couldn't tell. The thumping was certainly getting louder. Closer. As though all that rumble of noise was just outside the room.

Sal stared at the door. It was too dark to see the outline clearly, but a little of the street light from the narrow kitchen window glinted off the four yellow chain-locks, and those glints shimmered as the chains gently shook to the noises in the hallway.

The sound of the feet passed by. They faded. At length they were gone entirely.

After that there was silence. It lasted a long while. Though still Sal sat up in bed, gazing at the door. He wondered if he could hear whispers. He wondered if he could hear distant traffic, or whether his ears merely pulsed with a slow shushing of fluid.

Sal groped for the torch he kept beside the bed. He didn't yet dare put it on. In the darkness he crept to the door and listened. He reached out his hand and touched the cool metal of the chains, ensuring they were all securely in place. He went over to the wardrobe and crawled through on his hands and knees, into the warm damp musty room where Megan still slept in her precarious liquid form.

Sal clicked on his torch. He pointed it lazily into each corner of the room. He swung its fine beam briefly over Megan, her whiteness suddenly stark, her skin's translucency catching and holding that brightness; fading once the light had passed on by.

Sal went to sit with her, making sure he wasn't too close in case his weight upon the couch upset Megan's own weight and caused her to tumble to the floor.

With his torch off Sal now sat and stared. He waited for his eyesight to adjust. He wondered why it was that Megan glowed, even though the glow was very faint. It might have been something inside her. Or perhaps her hard pale shell simply caught what fine particles of light made their way into the room, holding them much better than the dullness of the walls.

Sal wanted to stay. He wanted to sleep in Megan's company. But it was not sensible.

'Because if they come. If they get in. They'll find me not there. So they'll search further. And they'll find us both here instead. They'll find us together.'

Sal moved back through to the main room.

He closed up the hidden door. He arranged the clothes in the wardrobe. He switched on the radio, setting it at its lowest volume.

'...*with the planktonic as well as the nektonic both having their place within the ocean, where to drift with the current is no less a means for survival than to have the ability to swim freely...*'

Sal positioned and steadied the little machine on the floor just beside the mattress, then lay himself down once again.

16. A Visitation

There were noises in the hallway, a soft scratching at the door. A small noise, though all the more prominent for the door itself being Sal's.

And Sal was awake at once, sitting upright in bed, peering hard through the blue-grey gloom of early morning, his insides pulsing and trembling.

Tentatively he reached out beside him and turned the low murmur of radio off to hear the noise better, though still he kept his fingers on the volume knob, ready to turn it up loud if anyone did force their way into the apartment.

The faint scrabbling sound continued. It was insistent. It had purpose. It grew more earnest for a moment. It stopped. It began again. Eventually Sal heard the lock of the door slipping open, followed by a gentle clink as the first of the chains was pulled taut. The door was pushed forward a second time, hard against the chain. The lock held fast.

A confused muttering came from the hallway.

'Oh. But I thought—' The chain was tested again, though not as forcefully. 'Hello?'

The door was pulled shut.

After a moment there was a knock. Polite but firm. Then the voice again. More assured this time. Speaking loudly through the closed door.

'Anybody in? I didn't actually intend—I wasn't

expecting this place to be—' The voice cleared its throat and tried once more. 'This is an official visit. I'm running an inspection of the building. I have the proper documentation. We received a call. We were informed. I won't take much of your time but—it would be very helpful. If I'd known this apartment was occupied. My name is Augustine. If you could just—'

The inspector stopped, hearing the chains now being undone one by one. The light was on as the door opened, fully this time. And there was Sal. The inspector stood looking at him for a brief moment.

'Oh.'

He squinted past Sal, on into the room, then back down at the boy.

'I see. I didn't. Right. And what exactly—' He paused. He took a breath. 'And does Madox know you're here?'

'It's not mine. I'm just looking after it. I'm renting.'

Sal stepped back, allowing Augustine to enter.

'I'm trying it out. Living alone. It's what people do. I wanted to try. To see.'

Sal closed the door and applied the first of the chains. He moved down to do the second, then left it hanging.

The inspector glanced quickly round the room, taking in the details in an instant. As he turned back towards the larval he smiled.

'You should have told me, Sal.' The smile broadened. 'I'm glad. I really am. Impressed even. But you might have told me. I'd have helped you. I'd have been happy to. There are much better places than this around. Better neighbourhoods. I could have found you somewhere.

You'd have been safer. No need for all those flimsy locks.'

'This is fine. I like it. I'm just trying. I'm happy with this.'

Now that he was up Sal went to make breakfast. He looked in the cupboard and brought out a small fresh packet of coffee which he showed to the inspector, who nodded casually. But as Sal began to make it the inspector moved forward with quick steps, and before Sal could protest Augustine had opened the very same cupboard and peered inside. Sal thought to reach up and push the door closed, but it wouldn't have helped. In any case the inspector, having had a good look at the cupboard's repetitive contents, merely nodded once again and closed the door.

'Not your normal fare. I thought you weren't so keen on all this rich food. I mean—coffee?'

'It's not for me. I'm only making it for you. I don't like it. It hurts.'

Sal tore the paper packet open and poured a large quantity of the powder into a small saucepan. Augustine did not interrupt his efforts.

'And yet you do have it. The food. It can't just be for guests.'

Sal didn't look round. He spoke slowly as he concentrated on his task.

'It's not all mine. Some of it was a gift. A moving-in present. I don't like to throw anything out. Don't like to be wasteful. And yes, for guests maybe.'

Augustine smiled again, this time unseen by Sal.

'You could always sell it. Or give it away. Lots of

people would appreciate it. Especially round these parts. The things some people will do to get food. The lengths they'll go to.'

'No.' Sal rummaged for a mug and began to pour what he'd brewed into it. 'I don't think so. I don't know.'

He presented the mixture to the inspector, then went about preparing his own meal, a warm barley mash, pre-soaked, into which he now sliced a large over-ripe banana.

'I think I'll keep it all. For now. It keeps well.' He concentrated on his cutting, making each slice the same width. 'But you said there was a break-in? Has something happened?'

The inspector was back by the door, his coffee held lightly in one hand. He was examining the chains. He was testing their strength and that of their housing. He turned round with a vague, tired expression.

'Yes—well, no.' He lifted the cup to his lips but didn't drink. 'Not really. Nothing of much interest.'

'But someone called you?'

'Just a disturbance in the night. You've no need to worry.'

'I did hear something.' Sal had sat down with the bowl of mash on his lap, but now he looked up eagerly. 'Yes. I think I heard. I could help this time. Really help. I could match it up. What I heard in the night. I could match it to the scene. To all the information you've been given.'

Augustine sighed.

'There's really not much to see. Or to know. It was a break-in. Very boring really. Someone got pretty shook up by it. You know, properly scared. Nothing much more than that though.'

'I thought I heard a scream. I wasn't sure. But now I'm sure. Someone screamed in the night.'

'Maybe so. She may well have screamed. Yes. She—called us later. She let us know. But it's cleared up now. A straightforward case. She won't be wanting any further fuss.'

'Who was it? What did they do?'

'Just some larvals. They may have expected a nest. That sort of thing. You get them in these parts. It's common enough. It's easier that way for them to get at food. Luxuries and such.' The inspector waved a hand vaguely. 'All sorts. You know. You don't need to worry about it. They won't come back.'

'But they attacked her? And she's alright?'

'They're an odd bunch, these types. They wouldn't have expected what they found. They were probably pretty startled. You know? More scared than she was herself. And they have their own weird sort of ethics. They wouldn't rob or attack another larval. No no. Nor an adult, for that matter, not even a young one. But had they found eggs, or perhaps something more than merely eggs—'

The inspector glanced around the room, his eyes lingering briefly on the wardrobe before moving on.

'To them that'd be fair game, see? So if they were to find someone in a pupal state, well, that's almost the same. They'd regard such a person as not quite living and not quite dead. And they'd have a point too. Even the law is a little hazy on that particular detail. Yes indeed. Something we're trying hard to change. But it's not that easy. The arguments are not easy. And then, with all history against you, well—'

He sipped at his coffee. He grimaced. He tried to suppress the expression, transforming the grimace into a tight-lipped grin.

Sal wasn't watching.

'But you didn't find anything. So you came to my door. You tried to open it. You used your bit of plastic. I heard it. So will you try other doors? Other people in the building?'

Augustine sat down on the sofa. He gave a broad smile, showing his neat white teeth.

'It's really good to see you, Sal. And looking so well. You should eat more, you know? I never felt Madox fed you quite enough. He was always good to you, of course, just a little stingy on the food front. But now you're out on your own. You should relax. And eat well. Eat a good lot. It'll help you to sleep better. It really will. *Eat well to sleep well*. That's what they say. That's what we have on our pamphlets.'

Sal took another spoonful of mash. He sucked on a slimy chunk of banana. He nodded thoughtfully.

'I'm okay for now. I'm just trying things out. I'm seeing what it's like.'

'Of course, of course. And how—how did you find this place? This building. And why here, exactly? Why this area?'

'I didn't. Someone else did. It was a suggestion. I wasn't

looking. Not really. It was sort of sudden. Someone said something. So I decided.'

'And Madox?'

'I decided on my own. Madox won't mind. He hasn't said anything. He hasn't said I can't.'

Augustine nodded, smiling once again as he glanced at the bathroom door then smoothly back towards the wardrobe.

'You know all the apartments in this building are roughly the same, yes? All fairly dull, simple spaces. Not exactly the same, of course, but—pretty similar.'

Sal shook his head. Augustine looked at him closely as he went on.

'Anyone would know that, you see? If they visited. Anyone knowing would see that. And from what I've seen today, well, I'd say this place is a little smaller than most. Just a little on the small side. That's all.'

There was no reaction from Sal. He went on sucking at and swallowing his mash. Augustine nodded.

'I hope you're not paying too much for it though. You shouldn't be. Not for a place like this. For such a small space. I could find you somewhere better. So much better. Easily. Match the cost even. Wouldn't be a problem. Somewhere nicer. Bigger. Somewhere less—noisy. At night. Maybe. If that was something you wanted.'

'I'm happy here. Just where I am. Thank you.'

Augustine smiled and glanced pointedly over his shoulder.

'That's a good wardrobe. Is it sturdy? It looks a little cheap. Is it cheap? It seems fairly basic. No frills. But that's no matter so long as it's sturdy. It'd take a while to shift, I'm guessing.'

'I don't need to move it. Thank you. I like it where it is.'

'Of course. Yes. I get it. I hear you. But if you did ever need help, Sal. Or even just a new wardrobe. A bigger one. Heavier. Sturdier. Anything. Well, you know where I am, right?'

'Thank you. It's fine. I'm fine. Thank you.'

Augustine sat staring at him for a moment longer. Then abruptly he stood. He drained his coffee, breathed in sharply through his teeth, and set the empty mug on the table.

'I need to get on, Sal. And you'll need to start your day. But you'll let me visit, yes? Now that I know you're here? Yes. I think—I will do just that. I'll visit from time to time. If you like. If you don't mind.'

'I don't mind. But—'

Augustine waited, brow raised.

Sal continued hesitantly.

'But if I'm not here. You won't. You wouldn't—'

The inspector's brow dipped.

'Won't wouldn't what?'

'Won't come in.'

'If you have those chains on, Sal, I won't disturb you. I may knock. To check. But of course, yes, I'll respect your privacy. And they look to be good chains. I admire the job you've done on them. You could get a better lock, of course. I could help with that. I have the proper equipment. Good tools. Professional.'

'But if I was out. Then the chains—' Sal squirmed a little, struggling for the right phrase. 'I can't put them across when I'm out. And I don't want you—I wouldn't want you—'

'Ah, I see now!' The inspector laughed. 'Of course, Sal, of course! Well, *if you're out*, then yes—no, I won't sneak inside and snoop around your personal domain. Your own little nest. No, no. I may be an inspector. Sure. I'd have the right. But no, you've my word on that, Sal. And yet a better lock. An extra lock. Externally operated. Mortised. With a key. That'd help. That'd really help. And I could help with that. I can help, Sal. That might make you feel—a little easier, perhaps.'

'I have to be careful. I don't want to cause any fuss. I don't want to attract attention.'

Augustine quietened at this.

'Of course, of course. You're right. No, I understand. I do understand. But I'll keep an eye on you. You know? Check you're okay? And I'll check the area too. I want you to be well, after all. I do want that.' He turned to go. 'And eat. Remember that. Don't skimp on your health now. Eat well and eat broadly. *Eat well to sleep well*. That's what they advise.'

'Thank you. And the disturbances?'

'Oh, don't you worry about them. I'll look into them. They're just little scares. Some old larval down the hall heard a scream. Someone got a shock. That's all.'

Augustine undid the top chain on the door. He examined the housing more closely. He ran his thumb over the bent nails.

Sal came to stand beside him, watching him.

'And she's alright?'

'Who?'

The inspector tugged gently at the chain.

'Whoever screamed.'

The inspector stopped and turned to Sal.

'Yes—she's fine now. I'll get the mess all cleared up today. She'll be quiet now. I'll let you get on. You wouldn't want to be getting involved in this sort of thing. You just—you just take care, alright? That's all that matters.'

The inspector gave another short surreptitious tug upon the chain, and departed.

LATE PHASE

The room was not entirely without light.

From where the small square window had been pasted over with newspaper there now came a yellow-grey glow from the strength of dawn sunlight pushing through from outside. The square itself was further patched in browns and dirty oranges by the irregular overlapping of the sheets, and all of it thinly striped with dark criss-crossing lines of text.

The floor of the room was bare but it was clean. There were no fine swirls of dust in the room's warm air, nor had any dust settled on the small single couch in one corner.

The wall adjacent to the window showed a door that was not quite closed. It hung open no more than an inch yet no spill of light came from the gap.

The glow from the window fell in a dim yellow square on the wall opposite, angling its shape over the top edge of a thick-set radiator. The radiator was turned up high and faint wavering shadows showed in the lit patch of wall just above, where the rising heat interfered with the path of the light.

A deep plastic tray lay below the radiator, a powdery residue lining its inside. There were other such trays about the room, these still held a little moisture where small puddles had collected in the shallow dints of the moulding.

The air of the room was dry. The couch had been shoved back against the wall that received the least light from the newspapered window. Tucked into the dimmest corner of the couch was a fat greyish object, roughly oval in form.

The object resembled a crude misshapen figure, its knees drawn up to its chest and its large head lowered. Its skin had wrinkled and hardened in the heat but even now there was movement beneath. The object pulsed, slowly, each gentle expansion stretching the skin still more. Fine cracks in its tough upper layer were beginning to show.

The noise outside the window: an unceasing distant hum, a quiet wash of city noise. Beyond the room's barely open door: a low murmur, as of surreptitious conversation. Inside the room: only silence.

When a deep split formed in the side of the hard pale skin it made no sound. The object continued to pulse as slowly and as regularly as before. Yet now, within this new grey split, a finer darker seam was visible.

At moments the pulsing would turn to a sudden strained convulsion, the whole object contracting deeply, with the wrinkles in the surface being then at their most pronounced. After this the tough grey rubbery membrane would stretch taut once again as what lay inside unwound still further, pushing against the flexible crust of its casing.

The new split increased in length, its lower point extending down towards the raggedy seat of the couch. A smooth second surface now showed clear within the widening gap. It glistened wetly in the day's soft yellow light, its pale brown tones lying stark against the dull grey of its shell.

Another large convulsion, and most of a back emerged. The back was streaked over with gold.

The gold was thicker at the top. It lay like overlapping sheets of leaf that separated lower down into finer veinings, into flattened wires of metal, each tapering to an imperceptible point.

Following this great exertion there came a period of rest. The slow insistent pulsing continued as before, the gold and brown of the back gently expanding, gently shrinking as it protruded awkwardly from the body-wide split.

When at length it came, the next great heave distorted the object beyond definition, its front buckling inward, its back bulging out into the fullness of its torso, though the head itself stayed submerged, tilted forward, resting on the spot where the knees had once been, tucked up as if still asleep, as if the emerging form was acting out its struggle, its desperate contortions, from deep within a dream.

Now the front of the greyness drew inwards completely as the figure strained to extract itself from itself, pulling at its own trapped limbs without having anything to pull against, no pivot point, no leverage. The glistening back rippled with the contortions of bone and muscle under its new wet skin. Only when a single arm had been unwrapped from its tight grey sock could the whole form relax for a while.

Calmly now this lone arm twisted itself inward once more, delving deeper inside the thick unyielding folds till it found its opposite shoulder. Bit by bit the other arm was eased backward, one hand holding the clinging greyness away as the new limb was gently drawn out.

Two hands, now free, felt for and lifted off the top flap of the shell, peeling it forward to reveal the head, still tilted forward, and covered all over in that same thickness of plated gold that wound and spread and thinned down the length of the back.

The head lolled itself slowly upright and stayed there, wavering slightly, gauging its own weight, its new soft-necked balance. The eyes remained closed. At moments the head would nod forward again and at once correct itself, as if trying always to return to the familiarities of sleep but halted from doing so by some far stronger impulse.

A body both weary and weak, though the hands held strength enough, pushing forward now more easily, half-sliding half-rolling the stubborn grey coverall from legs that slowly, difficultly, straightened themselves. Till the knees were uncovered. Till the ankles were uncovered. The soft humped mouldings of each foot. Till there was only a little of the greyness sticking to the tips of each toe. And the arms were straining forward, reaching out, easing and pulling and tugging. Till the thick rubbery casing was finally unstuck and hung swaying, for just a brief moment, from the sure light grip of fingers that soon, carelessly, let that last corner fall, onto the threadbare cushions of the couch.

Then the gilded figure unfurled itself just a little bit further, stretching out to lie full length on top of the tatters of greyness, utterly exhausted.

•

The distorted square of light, cast from the window's glow, had crept gradually round the walls. Now its lower edges fell upon the face lying at the far end of the couch.

It was a soft light, it gave no more warmth than the room already provided, but still the girl's eyes twitched beneath their lids. Then the lids themselves smoothly, gummily, opened, and two deep blue irises thickened as they adjusted to the new comparative brightness.

The girl drew her head backward, out of the reach of the glow. Slowly she eased herself upright. She felt faint. She brought her long bony legs up to her chest and wrapped her narrow arms around them. Her chin she lightly rested on her knees.

Only her eyes moved, swivelling first towards the source of the light, blinking at the orange-brown square of the window and its patched and crisscrossed covering. Then for a long while she gazed at the dark doorway, getting a sense of its shape, its odd deceptive angle.

She puzzled at how it remained ever so slightly open. She couldn't tell why but she expected it at any moment to swing back freely on its hinges. Yet it stayed unaccountably fixed. She extended a leg and touched her toes to the bared floorboards. Taking care with her new unfamiliar weight she rose to her feet. She stood wavering.

Something clung to her behind. Something had stuck itself to her and didn't want to let go. An extra small weight. She plucked the dry grey skin once again from herself, watching as the two materials, the old and the new, pulled against each other, stretching, till the one came free and sagged in her hand, and the other sprang back to its tautness, its new roundness.

She held the old skin up before her. A rag of grey, cracked and torn, one side perfectly smooth, the other dry and flaking. She tried to find a shape within the folds but there were no clear features left that she could make out. She dropped the object to the floor.

The door intrigued her. She stepped slowly over to it with a gait half-wobbled half-determined. Gingerly she put her hand through the dark gap and ran her fingers down the inside of the door till she touched upon a thin chain. She felt for and unhooked it. If someone had intended to lock her inside they'd made a poor job of it. She stepped back to let the door swing open.

Here now was a new darkness, a softness that she stepped up into and through, ducking forward between heavy cloth, between a muted jangle of hangers, to find another door. This one had no catch on her side. With barely a shove it swung outwards and she winced in the full light of the small pristine room that opened before her. Holding up her hand before her eyes she stepped down into the new bright space.

She felt she knew this room, but not as it now stood. It didn't quite have the arrangement she would have expected. And it was silent. It shouldn't have been silent. She bowed to a small radio and turned it on.

'...*located high in the abdominal cavity, each one ageing as she ages, and only stimulated into further development once the threshold of appropriate nutrients...*'

Wincing once more, this time at the painful sharpness of the voice, she swiftly turned the radio off again.

She moved to the refrigerator. An instinctive action. It wasn't as well stocked as she remembered, but there was still plenty to choose from. She selected a bar of chocolate. With her fingertip she split the foil, smiling all the while she drew the curve of her nail down the bar's long length. Lifting the chocolate to her lips she nibbled at its sweetness.

Still eating she went to the bathroom. She tried the cord for the light. The harshness of its bulb was too much to bear, so she pulled the cord again, relying instead on the natural light coming in through the doorway. She stood facing the mirror. A fan heater was attached to the wall. She clicked its dial round all the way and let its flood of hot air wash over her.

There was gold about her head. It rested upon her like a long metallic cap, like a close-fitting hood that stretched down across her shoulders and over her back. The density of the gold was more prominent higher up and thinned ever further into little flicks and curls the lower down it reached till it became so thin it merged at last and faded into the soft brown of her skin.

She dabbed at the gold. It was cool to the touch. It shifted under her fingertips, little patches loosening. It looked like gold foil but it felt like cold wet silk. Her skin too still felt damp. It felt vaguely sticky, enveloped in a shimmering clinging mucosa. But this fine film soon began to dry in the heat from the fan and as she brushed at it it fell away from her skin in minute silvery flakes.

Then slowly, in the hot dry air, the gold itself began to separate its layerings and veinings, its flicks and its curls, into individual strands too fine to be seen, which first shivered and glittered then lifted and swirled back up and around her shoulders while she stood, contentedly, watching herself in the mirror, and every so often taking small bites from the chocolate.

18. Easing In

There were people on the pavement ahead of Sal as he returned home from work. He slowed his step to put some distance between him and them, even though the people never once turned round.

The bus stop was busy as he approached it. Sal hung back till the next bus came then hurried on past with his hands pocketed and his shoulders hunched. None of the seated passengers glanced his way.

When he arrived at the entrance to Megan's building Sal lingered outside the glass frontage. He turned carelessly upon the spot till he was sure no one else was about before ducking inside between the jammed-open panes of the door.

Sal softened his footfalls up the stairs. Sal paused at every echoed click, every creak from above or below. Sal peeked round corners. Sal checked the hallway was empty before shuffling along it to the apartment, his key already tight between his fingers.

He knew the precise quirks of the door and its lock, how to angle the key so its teeth turned in the grooves without catching, how to lift the weight of the door through its handle and swing it inwards in such a manner that the hinges didn't squeak, how to do up each inner chain with only the barest of clinks. Every action precise. Every precaution of utmost importance.

But the room Sal now turned round to see did not

look right. He'd left it in a carefully executed state of use. Cushions had been expertly indented. An unwashed bowl and spoon had been left on the table, a dribble of milk within both. The corner mattress had been lightly rumpled, the bedclothes loosely folded down to air. He'd hung an unironed shirt on the door of the wardrobe, hoping to dissuade potential intruders from thinking there was anything more than merely clothes inside. The tub in the bathroom had been wetted, the mirror misted, the door closed to keep in the moisture till Sal returned.

But now the bathroom door was ajar and the light was on. Now there was not just his bowl and spoon on the table but a littering of opened biscuit packets and empty tins, a sticky trail that led back to the raided cupboards. His unmade bed was a mass of lumpy sheets. His precariously balanced shirt had fallen and lay crumpled under the wardrobe door, wedging it open.

Sal tightened his grip on the key still poised between his fingers. He stepped cautiously towards the wardrobe. He knelt at its edge to crawl through between the heavy coats and dresses.

The inner door was unlatched. Wide open. Sal took the small pencil torch from his pocket to shine into the darkness of the room. He angled it at once towards the couch, to the corner where the palely cocooned Megan should have glowed back at him in the thin beam of blue-white light. There was nothing. Sal blundered awkwardly backwards through the wardrobe on hands and knees and stood up. He stayed very still.

The space had changed once more. His bedclothes, no longer heaped in the middle of the mattress, were now partly vertical. They were turned his way. Something tawny, something topped with soft fine gold, was facing him. They were listening attentively to the sounds that had woken them, and they considered Sal with sleepy wide blue eyes.

•

This stranger, this young adult, this interloper of a girl, now slowly stood, unbending herself from the bedclothes. She was wearing a long cotton nightshirt, striped in pink and blue, holding it protectively closed before her.

She was taller than Sal, the hard foam mattress upon which she stood making her taller still so that she had to stoop to look at him, her shoulders tensing inward, warily.

She swayed a little from foot to foot, keeping her balance, her eyes narrowing, her head tipping now to one side. She glanced down to where Sal still gripped the key, held out defensively before him. The girl stared at the key, then around at the apartment, then back at Sal's glistening small black eyes.

'Oh, Sal.' She stepped sideways from the bed. 'This was all you? All this—mess?' She gestured vaguely at the chaos of the room. 'I didn't even know you knew. Did someone tell you? Did I tell you? No, I couldn't have. I wouldn't have. So then—how? Oh, my dear Sal.'

She came forward and half-fell half-folded herself around the larval, letting him take her weight.

Sal stood rigid, his chin raised to perch upon the girl's shoulder, his black eyes gazing through a veil of golden hair. The girl's thick sleepy smell was filling his head. The strength of her hard bony arms was restricting his breath.

Sensing his discomfort she relaxed her hold, though she didn't let go, as now she poured out her explanation.

'I couldn't say, though. I just couldn't. You do understand that, yes? You know I couldn't. It's not advised. I wanted to. I kept trying to make up a good reason to.'

Her voice reverberated through the softness of Sal's body. It buzzed. It made him itch.

'But they say that telling anyone, no matter how close a friend, they say it's always such a risk. Because then you'd have felt responsible. You'd have had that burden too. So I couldn't. I should have. I see that. But what if having done so—'

She let go of him and stood back.

'What if you didn't approve? I thought you might not. And I didn't want that argument. I couldn't bear it. So I thought that maybe if I just—and then maybe one day you too—'

She smiled and shook her head.

'But it doesn't matter. Here you are! And look at this place. I did wonder. Today. When I woke up. And I was all in a daze. I didn't know who I was! But how long have you—and how long was I—'

She stopped. Sal's eyes were no longer meeting hers, and she was no longer holding her nightshirt closed.

'Oh. Yes. Of course. I imagine it must be quite a shock. I hadn't thought. I'm sorry. I didn't mean—'

She took another step back, folding and gripping the cotton closed once more. Sal's eyes flicked back upward. He stared at her, blinking, blank-faced.

Slowly Megan relaxed. She breathed out. Then in one easy movement she shrugged the nightshirt from her shoulders and let it fall to her wrists, cinching the material in around her waist as slowly she turned on the spot, allowing Sal to look at her from all angles.

'It's true. I know what you're thinking.'

Her voice was easy, matter-of-fact.

Sal didn't move.

After one full revolution Megan drew the shirt back over her shoulders and began doing up the buttons. She leant forward as she did so, as if to share a deep secret, as if she didn't want anyone else to hear.

'But it *is* quite incredible, don't you think? I sort of knew it would be. Though I didn't quite expect *this*. Well, I don't really know what I did expect. But when I saw, when I went to the mirror, I just stood and stared. Stared and stared. After all, what else would you do? What would anyone do? Was it me? I mean, how much of me was still me? I couldn't tell for sure. I couldn't remember! There might have been something important about me I'd forgotten. I mean in how I thought. But what did any of that matter? There I was! And the biggest strangeness of all was that it didn't feel strange.

The woman in the mirror didn't *seem* like a stranger. I moved, she moved. What could be more *me* than that? But then I—'

With a sudden swift lunge Megan took Sal by the hand. He didn't flinch.

'Come.'

She led him to the sofa and made him sit. She flopped down beside him, leaning back lazily against the cushions while Sal sat stiffly before her.

'So, go on. Tell me what happened. Tell me everything.'

Sal was silent for a moment. He blinked nervously.

'What do you want to know?'

'Oh, I don't mind, everything. Tell me when you knew. How you found out. All that stuff. You know—everything.'

Megan reached for a box of biscuits, rattling out its last crumbs onto the floor. She reached for another box and tore its top open, her fingernails ripping easily through the soft cardboard. Then she froze. A biscuit halfway to her mouth. Sal was staring at her hands.

Megan tilted the box towards him.

'Want one? I've got lots. Oh, what am I saying, you probably stocked these yourself! Have you been spending your money on me? I hope not. Or not too much in any case. But come on now. Tell me.'

Sal tentatively accepted a single biscuit. He sucked on it to soften it. Then, breathing in deeply, he began. He told her everything. How he'd found out what she was doing. How he used to follow her. How he'd wanted to warn her, to dissuade her. How he had looked after her.

He went through the minutiae of his routine. His daily ruse. His nighttime fears.

Megan listened attentively, crunching through biscuit after biscuit. A whole packet gone in just a few minutes. And then, having finished all that were to hand, she got up to go to the cupboards.

'Don't stop. I'm still listening.'

She came back with a tin of condensed milk and a spoon. She peeled back the stiff metal lid.

Only on one occasion did she properly interrupt Sal's narrative.

'Wait. What was it like? In there, I mean. What was it like seeing me?'

Sal hesitated. He considered the matter deeply.

'You were very quiet.'

'Well, yes. But what did I—what does it, look like? I've only seen the casing. The skin. It was gruesome. Such a floppy dead thing. It's still through there. I think I'll keep it. For a bit. Do you want to see it? I'll go get it.'

'No.'

Sal stopped her in the act of standing.

'I saw. I mean—it was difficult. How quiet you were. But you were there. I knew you were there, always, in there. Even if I couldn't see you. It wasn't like sleep. It was something else. But so quiet. And when I'd clean you, it was—'

He stared at her, the bright black of his eyes locked fiercely on the big deep blue of hers. Megan stopped eating for a moment.

Sal swallowed.

'It was like a memory. Of you. And frightening. How easy it was. Just to leave you. It wasn't right. I wanted to do more. But I couldn't. Not to you. But I filled up the buckets and emptied the trays. And sometimes I'd wash you. With a cloth. Dampened. I didn't need to. I don't think it made any difference. So I stopped that. And it was as easy to stop as it was to go on. It didn't matter either way. You were still there. Still so quiet. None of it mattered.'

Megan took another slow spoonful of condensed milk, watching Sal all the while.

'And did you want me to wake up? When you touched me? Did you want me to move? To break out?'

Sal nodded.

'And did you want me never to change? To be just that way for ever more? Easy and quiet and just a memory?'

Again he nodded.

'And how about now? Are you pleased? Pleased for me? Do you think it was, perhaps, after all that, worth the effort?'

'I don't know.' Sal glanced downwards. 'I don't know.'

Megan placed the unfinished tin on the table. Leaning forward across the couch she embraced Sal, awkwardly, squeezing him to her.

When she released him and sat back his expression had not changed.

'Oh, Sal. Come on. It's not like we've never seen an adult before. Just not me as one. And look at this!'

She took a big handful of golden hair in her fist.

'I didn't think there would be so much of the stuff.

Not at first. Not all at once. I thought I'd have to grow it. And this colour! I mean, is this even a colour? And look at my teeth!'

She curled her lips back top and bottom briefly.

'And my nails. And my eyes. None of it's all that unfamiliar. I mean, we recognise such things, but then, when it's your own, you suddenly wonder, I mean really wonder. What's it all for? Because I don't really feel any different. I still feel just as much me. But now with all these things. These extras. Plus I had to check for any deformities. It's advised. Things can go wrong, you see. There's a checklist. I had it sort of memorised. But oh— wait there!'

Megan hopped from the couch and darted on tiptoes across to the wardrobe.

'I had to hide this. Didn't want to lose it. I hope you've not been through my pockets!'

She came back to the couch and flopped down beside the larval, a flimsy well-used pamphlet clutched in her hand. She flicked idly through it without looking.

'There's lots of other useful information too. What diet you should be on leading up to pupation. How to create the right humidity. What documents you need for registration. All standard guidance, of course. But crucial to get it right. I mean, really important.'

She thrust the raggedy pamphlet out towards Sal. He took it but didn't look at it, just held it.

'What about after? What about—' Sal shifted uncomfortably. 'Social interactions.'

Megan pointed the tip of her spoon at the pamphlet.

'It's all in there. There's a long paragraph on it. There are diagrams. I tried to learn it all before I—well, before I started the change. But it's a bit weird. I thought it might make sense later. You know, after.'

Sal glanced down at the pamphlet. He opened it slowly. He turned a few pages.

'And what about—' He looked up. 'Other things?'

'Oh, yes. Plenty of other things.' Megan rubbed her eyes. 'It's all in the pamphlet.' She stood up smartly. 'You should read it. Take it away with you. I don't mind. Just don't lose it. You can bring it back when you next visit.'

Megan stretched her long arms out to either side. She yawned, wide-mouthed, her white teeth showing. Then she held out her hand, palm upwards. Sal looked at it.

'Keys, of course.' Megan stared at him expectantly. 'I'm just so very tired, Sal. I'm sorry. I think that happens. I think it probably lasts for a while, too. I'm so very grateful though. Really I am.'

Sal stood and gently placed the key in her hand, along with its glow-worm fob. Megan smiled and hugged him tightly once more.

'Come tomorrow? Or no, maybe the next day. Yes, that'd be better. Perhaps I'll have more strength in me by then. All I really want to do now is eat and sleep and eat and sleep and eat! Not a lot of fun for you. But there's still so much for us to talk about, at some point.'

Sal felt himself being ushered to the door. Then he was outside it and Megan was whispering to him through the already closing gap.

'And don't tell anyone. I don't suppose it really matters so much now, people knowing. But I'd prefer to keep quiet about it for just a bit longer, yes? Till I'm more settled? Till things aren't quite so—new.'

Sal nodded.

Megan smiled.

The door was shut.

Sal stood for a time in the dark corridor, trying to listen for noises, trying to imagine what she might now be doing in there.

Then he remembered the spyhole. He didn't look at it. He didn't want her to think he'd realised she might be watching him.

He walked away. It would be the first night in a long while that he'd be staying again at his father's house.

19. Unfamiliarities

There was a faint popping sound, an irregular metallic ticking, a gurgling, a hiss.

Megan felt she knew that noise. She had lived with it, woken up to it, lain quiet and still, listening to it, for weeks. Perhaps longer. Perhaps all her life. And she had wondered at it, questioned it, but had never been able to discover what it was, had never had the ability to investigate its source.

But now she was brighter, more alert. Now she was able to open her eyes. She could sit up in bed through the last blue-greys of the night as it shifted imperceptibly into morning, and she could hear the hiss of the boiler flame, and the gurgle and pop of the hot water as it coursed through the pipes and into the radiators. She could hear the metals expanding as they warmed.

She didn't have any idea how long she'd slept. She didn't even know what day it was. She felt hungry and she felt cold. She turned on the pocket-sized radio for company.

'...being perceived in many cases as an ancestral relic, their use having slowly shifted throughout history, and any aesthetic qualities likewise linked to such...'

She went to run a bath. She sat on the edge of the tub, stirring the water idly with her toes, while making her way through a stack of wafery biscuits and a large freshly-opened tube of fish paste.

She left the bathroom door ajar as she stretched herself out in the hot water, allowing the steam to plume up to the ceiling and spread through into the main room.

'…*in producing and exuding an opaque sugar-syrup laced with vital minerals that serve as the perfect foodstuff for early…*'

She had all the proper bathtime accoutrements. They were of the cheaper sort, but she had them. They came in plain white boxes; a bathroom set she'd bought in preparation. From one cardboard packet: a new bar of scented pink soap. From another: an oblong of dark yellow sponge.

'…*where such a function has in some cultures been exploited through the prolongation of such metabolic industry by the persistence of…*'

The sponge was very stiff, retaining its firmness even after Megan held it under water between her knees, squeezing and pumping and hissing out its air. It scored shallow grooves into the wetted bar of soap. Megan didn't mind rubbing this coarseness against her new skin. She liked it. She liked that she could be rougher on herself without worrying about snags and sudden bloodless tearings.

'…*a factory internalised, the excess body-heat produced allowed to dissipate evenly through each of the dermal layers, creating a thermal glow that can often be evident at close…*'

She didn't really need to scrub herself. She didn't feel especially dirty. Still she let the sponge make its own minute scratches over her skin. She searched out every new part of herself, every little corner, every crevice. She soft-scratched them too.

'...through weaning at the earliest opportunity in order to maximise yields from extended production, though this may in itself effect a...'

Megan's skin had darkened with the hotness of the bath water, her blood straining beneath to let out excess heat. It darkened still further from the scratching of the sponge.

'...had soon become a commercial enterprise, the raw white syrup processed through boiling and crystallisation to be sold on as a delicacy, despite the likelihood of such produce...'

Megan examined her hands, letting the sponge float gently away from her. She paid close attention to her nails, those perfect little claws. Their tiny curving blades rooted firmly in each tapered fingertip.

'...being selectively bred for this purpose, both in regard to overall size and thereby natural storage capacity, as well as the reliability of individuals in which...'

She let her hair soak. She sank herself down low so the rim of the water bordered her upturned face. When she rose again her hair stuck to her shoulders and back, as it had when first she'd seen it. But the gold was duller now, heavied, muted with wetness.

'...contrary to being in servitude were lauded within their communities where the levels of fattening required had to be provided by the common...'

There were noises in the hallway. Megan could hear people moving past her door. People were stopping to talk. All that activity, and only the thickness of a single wall away.

'...due to the swelling that took place, discomfort would only be an issue when regular expression was not properly maintained and could itself lead to…'

There came a knock.

It was unmistakably someone knocking at Megan's own door. She sat up straight, but slowly, making no noise in the water, even holding her breath to stay quiet.

'…despite the reliability and availability of modern supplements having rendered this practice redundant the functional aspect persists and can still be…'

Another knock.

Megan eased herself out of the bath, trying to quieten the splash and suck as she did so. She wrapped a towel around her waist and buttoned on the shirt she'd worn in bed, before soft-stepping over to the radio and turning the volume lower till the machine at last clicked off.

There was no more noise now from the hallway. The knocking had stopped. Megan tried the spyhole. A man was stooping forward, leaning in very close to the door. Megan couldn't see him properly.

'Hello?'

The man jerked upright at the sound of Megan's voice. He stood listening, intently. In his hands he held a small grey square of plastic. This he turned between his fingers as he waited for another word. Then he looked directly at the spyhole.

'Sal?'

Megan shrank back. She considered the situation quickly then began undoing the chains, stopping just before the last was released. She opened the door and peered out at the man.

They stared at each other for a moment.

The man lifted his eyebrows, as though in disbelief at his own understanding.

'Sal?'

'He's not here.' Megan glanced down at the man's hands. The grey square of plastic had gone. 'He'll be at home, probably. Or at work. I don't know.'

'And this—this isn't his home?'

'This is my home.'

'Ah.' The man nodded slowly. 'Of course. I see now.' He smiled. 'An easy mistake. I'm sorry then to have disturbed you. I'll leave you be.'

He began to walk away.

'Wait.' The door was closed while the last chain was undone, then Megan opened it wide. 'Do you know him? Are you a friend of Sal's? He's my friend too, you see. He was staying here. He's been looking after me. The place, I mean. On my behalf. While I've been—'

She stopped.

The man looked at her and smiled once more.

'Away?'

'Yes. Away. That's right. But I'm back now.'

'I understand. I do understand. And you've nothing to fear from me. But I'd best be getting on. If you do happen to see Sal then perhaps mention I called? But—no. It's more likely I'll see him before you do.'

He sighed and began again to walk away.

'Wait.' Megan took a step out into the hall, one hand held behind her, gripping the jamb. 'You can come in if you like. That is, if you're a friend of Sal's. I don't mind.

It'd be nice to meet you. Because I don't—I don't really know anyone. And I have food. I could make you something.'

The man hesitated only briefly before returning. He stepped smartly forward, his hand outstretched.

'Augustine. And yes, I know Sal. I've known him for, well—for a good long time now.'

Megan barely took hold of the hand before going back inside, letting the man follow, leaving him to close the door himself.

'What do you like to eat? I have lots. Maybe you wouldn't like it though. I don't know. What do you like?'

'Oh, nothing. I won't stay long. It really was Sal I wanted to see. I wanted to—check he was well.'

'I think he is.'

'Though I suppose it doesn't much matter any more.'

'What?'

The man hesitated.

'You haven't told me your name.'

'Megan. But I'll have to change that now. I know it's not the done thing to keep one's old—'

She became suddenly very still.

'It's alright. It's quite alright.' Augustine shrugged, speaking in an easy offhand manner. 'I quite understand. And as I say, you've nothing to fear from me. From anyone in fact. But I do see. I understand. It's my job to—to notice things. I am an inspector, after all. Inspector Augustine? Perhaps Sal told you about me at some point?'

Megan remained very still. She was watching this man,

assessing him. She was shivering slightly. Her hair was still wet. It dripped down onto her shirt.

'You might want to dry that.' The inspector pointed. 'Brush it too. But gently. Make sure to be ever so gentle with it. It'll be that much weaker at first. Is it golden? It's not easy to tell when it's so wet.'

Megan nodded. She pinched at the wet fabric of the shirt and pulled it forward, away from herself, from where it had started to cling.

'Yes. That happens.' The inspector smiled. 'The gilding. It can be a shock. A pleasant shock. Though some still worry about public perceptions. Understandable, I suppose. They really ought to include something about that in the official literature. Hmm.' The inspector took out his notepad and began scribbling. He went on without looking up. 'Don't worry though. It does darken within the first few weeks or so. It'll find its natural colour. And you'll have to take care of it.' He put his pad away. 'And yourself.'

'I don't think I have a brush. I didn't know.' Megan glanced towards the bathroom. 'I'll need to buy one.'

Augustine considered this for a moment. Then he dug in his coat pockets, rummaged briefly, and produced a comb. He held it out to Megan.

'Here. You can have this. You can keep it. It's not new but it is clean. I always make sure it's very clean.'

Megan took the object from the inspector's out-stretched hand. The comb was pale yellow, almost see-through, with deep swirlings of white running through it. Augustine watched as she turned it delicately between her fingers, examining it. He answered the question he guessed she must be thinking.

'Horn. Animal horn. I don't actually know which animal. I don't suppose it matters. And it's nothing special. I have another somewhere.'

There were two teeth missing from one end. Megan ran her fingernail down the comb's short length, making it rasp, thinly. She tried pulling it through her hair, starting from the very top of her crown. The comb snagged almost at once.

'No, no, not like that! Never like that.'

Augustine came forward with such a rushed step, his hands reaching out, that Megan stepped back instinctively, but the inspector ignored her.

'And not while it's so wet. It'll be all muddled from when you soaked it. It's ever so fine at the moment, you see. And not all that strong. It'll tangle easily. You need to dab it dry first of all. And then you—here.'

He took the comb from her. Her fingers were limp, barely gripping the item. The inspector moved round behind her.

'Very gently at first. See? Start a little way from the bottom and then gradually work your way upwards till the comb begins to move freely. You'll soon get the hang of it.'

He continued for a moment, combing just the ends of the wet hair. Large drips gathered on the comb and fell onto Megan's shirt, soaking quickly into the already damp fabric. The inspector could smell the hot fresh warmth of her, mixed with the scent of cheap soap.

He swallowed hard. He shut his eyes tight and moved away. He gave her back the comb.

'Of course, you'll be embarrassed. I know. I quite understand. You don't need to do it right away. I'll be gone now. You take all the time you like. Just—don't force it, whatever you do.'

Megan stood dumbly. She looked at the inspector. She looked down at the comb in her hands.

The inspector assessed her concern.

'Do you have someone you can talk to? Someone to advise you? You must have had help to begin with.'

Megan nodded.

'Good. That's good. But if you do need more. More advice, I mean. And if you feel you can trust me—'

He took out his notepad again. He wrote down his details and raggedly tore off the page. He held it out at arm's length.

Megan took it without expression, holding the piece of paper in one hand, the comb in the other.

'I'll leave you be. You'll have plenty to be getting on with.' The inspector began backing towards the door. 'You'll need a new place to live, for one thing. Maybe somewhere new entirely. A new start. I could help with that. If you're interested. I know lots of people. Lots of towns.'

He lingered in the doorway, glancing briefly back into the room.

'It's a wonder. A real wonder you picked here, of all places. Why people so often go in for these sorts of locations, I'll never quite—' He smiled. 'But it's fine.

You did just fine. You got through it. Remember that. Some don't. For a wide variety reasons. Not all of them ghastly. Some just—don't. And no one's going to try and harm you now. They couldn't. Remember that too.'

'Thank you, Mr Augustine.'

'I think it's Sal you should be thanking. Perhaps. But—you're welcome, nonetheless.'

He left her. She heard his footsteps retreating, first in the hall and then the stairwell. And Megan stood, still dripping, still shivering, gripping her paper and comb.

And the paper she folded up small and placed into the damp top pocket of her shirt. And the comb she lifted slowly to her hair.

20. New Clothes

When Megan at last stepped cautiously outside she was relieved to see only larvals waiting at the bus stop. Nevertheless she hung back. She dawdled and dithered at the street corner, watching them from a distance.

It was the contradiction of her appearance that she was most concerned about, muffled as she was in cheap ill-fitting clothes. She'd pulled her old cap down as far as it would go, her fine gold hair bunched up and tucked beneath. A scarf was folded bulkily around her nose and mouth so that only her bright blue eyes were left peeping out.

The larvals were no more than a small grey knot, a blockage, in the otherwise empty corridor of the tall-walled red-bricked street. They moved only slightly, swaying as they waited. They did not talk to each other. They did not look at Megan.

When the bus appeared it came from Megan's direction and she walked briskly towards the stop as the vehicle overtook her. If the larvals chose at this moment to look her way she couldn't tell whether it was her now coming nearer that they noticed or just their natural inclination to stare at the approaching bus as it grumbled and squealed and hissed to a gentle stop.

The apparent ignorance of the larvals towards Megan was clarified by their making no move to allow her to board the bus first. There was no orderly queue. Megan added herself to the back end of their disordered huddling and shuffled on just as they did.

The conductor, having stepped down from the doors as they opened, was a larval himself. It was to be expected. He didn't pay any special attention to Megan either. He took her money and rolled off a ticket then stepped back up and onto the bus behind her.

Megan had hoped there might be a seat free up at the front so she could sit down at once and put her back to the other passengers. There wasn't. She had to walk on shakily down the aisle as the bus jerked forward, hoping all the while that the few larvals she passed would not look at her. And yet they did look, watching as Megan took her seat, before turning their tiny black-eyed glances aside to stare out the window at the tall red walls of the street as it rolled back and away.

Megan sat scrunched into herself. She retightened the scarf round her face, pulling it up as far as it would go. Perhaps the larvals hadn't noticed what she was. Perhaps they had and simply didn't care. Or perhaps, and she thought this far more likely, they had noticed all too quickly and yet didn't want to be seen to stare.

Megan couldn't recall if she'd ever acted this way herself. She tried hard to bring back an idea of how she'd actually felt when encountering adults. But where she expected a clear memory, an image, an instance, she found she could conjure only a sort of awareness, the vaguest of acknowledgements; no specific feelings were attached.

There had been a wide array of clothes in the wardrobe. Megan hadn't worried about what they were or where they came from when she'd bought them as a large secondhand bundle of oddments. She'd only wanted to fill up the wardrobe's ample interior, to pack it out as densely as she could. But wearing her old larval clothes for this her first proper outing hadn't felt right to her. They more or less still fitted but they felt too insubstantial, too flimsy, too dull. They felt now little more than undergarments. So Megan searched through and found a heavy shirt to put over them, and a large pair of men's trousers, and a long heavy coat to cover everything still further. It had seemed at the moment of putting all these layers on that to try and hide beneath them was the only way she could feel even partly at ease.

Of course, as soon as she stepped outside she decided otherwise. But there'd been something else mixed in with her embarrassment. There'd been a sense of her actually wanting the larvals to look, to wonder, to stare. And then, had they actually done so, she would have wanted to stare back. She would have wanted to glare. But they'd not afforded her such an opportunity and, when at length she stepped off the bus in the town centre, this mixture of opposing feelings had settled into one of general uncaring.

Even when Megan arrived at the shop, and entered, and lingered at the back because there was another adult presently being served, she felt strangely calm; at least in herself. And when this other adult did notice her, frowning briefly at her before exiting the shop, Megan didn't flinch, didn't feel the need to acknowledge the adult's confusion, let alone explain herself. She merely stepped forward to the front desk where the shop attendant stood eyeing her with quiet curiosity.

Megan removed her old cloth cap and lay it down on the counter in front of her.

'I thought, perhaps, that if you didn't recognise me, you might at least remember this.'

'Oh, I do.'

The attendant nodded. She picked up the cap and ran its worn and faded fabric between her fingers.

'And I think you should definitely keep hold of it. For posterity, or something. But as for the rest? Hmm.' She tipped her head to one side. 'Well, I was wondering if you'd let me throw the rest away. Or maybe incinerate it. At least then there wouldn't be any chance of it turning up some other day.'

'I need your help again.'

'I thought you might.'

'I can't afford much.'

'It's to be expected.'

'I feel bad asking.'

'You shouldn't. And there's really no need to worry.' She handed the cap back to Megan. 'You see, it sometimes happens that the clothes we get in from the factory have minor but irreparable faults in them.' She came out from behind the counter and leant back against it with her arms folded, gazing at Megan, getting the measure of her. 'Nothing you'd ever actually notice, of course, but it does tend to render the garments unsellable. At least at full price. A hefty discount is often permissible. It's either that or send the items back.'

'And what if the faulty clothes don't fit me?'

The attendant smiled.

'Then we may just have to find fault with a few that do.'

And she stepped to the main door and locked it, clacking the sign round to CLOSED.

21. THE NECESSARY PAPERWORK

The public area of the registration office was unaccountably small. The office itself was an out-of-the-way unnoticed sort of place, squashed between and below other offices, with its own poorly-marked entrance: a plain blue door in a narrow side alley. Inside, the cramped waiting room had just two chairs, squat and hard-cushioned, each positioned a short way from the high reception desk.

Beyond the desk was an open door through which came brief bouts of movement and low-level noise. This rear part of the office was where the actual work took place. It was staffed by larvals, though from reception it was impossible to see how many might be required for such work. Presently one of the larvals came through to continue their quiet business behind the front desk, keeping their head down, setting out and arranging certain unseen documents.

There was only one applicant in the waiting area. This fresh-faced girl sat forward in her chair, knees apart, bending low to rifle through a large square shopping bag that she steadied between the heels of her long brown boots. She wore a short jacket striped in lilac and mauve over a pale blue blouse of crumpled silk. Her lemon-yellow skirt had rucked backward over her knees as she bent forward to the bag. Her mass of long golden hair had flopped forward also, slipping from her shoulders, and she kept having to pause in her rummaging to push it back behind her ears.

Eventually she sat up, clutching a thick packet of string-tied papers, though she seemed reluctant to let go entirely of the shopping bag and remained slouching slightly forward, one hand gripping the bag's cloth handle, the other protectively covering the papers in her lap. She gazed at the larval who had come into the front office and who had not so much as glanced in her direction.

The larval was old. That was clear enough from the small limp folds in the grey-green skin around her neck, as well as the blotches of blueness on her cheeks. She also had a pair of black plastic spectacles perched back upon her head. The spectacles themselves didn't interest the girl so much as the baldness of the head on which they rested. There was nothing uncommon in this, but the girl now found herself briefly letting go of the papers in her lap in order to raise her hand to her own head, surreptitiously feeling the small tight shape of her skull as with her fingertips she combed the hair back over her scalp, letting it flop again lightly to one side.

To the girl there was something slightly obscene about the larval's baldness, though she couldn't recall having had such an opinion before. There was something un-nerving in the exposure it promoted. She felt a vague urge to walk over and poke the tip of a pen right into its smooth centre, just to see how easily it could be done.

'Be with you in two ticks.'

The old larval, still busy arranging papers behind the

desk, had not looked up as she spoke. But now, as she gathered a trio of folders and moved away again towards the back office, she glanced briefly at the applicant and sighed, letting her shoulders sag.

'Legs together, dear.' She gave a weary smile. 'It may only be me in here, but you ought to get used to such things.'

Then she bustled away through the inner door.

The girl shifted her bag, smoothed her skirt, and brought her knees neatly together. She tried crossing one leg over the other, but it felt uncomfortable, unnatural, with that awkward press of one knee into the back of the other. She thought perhaps she was doing it wrong, so she stood up and stepped forward to the front desk instead, pinning her shopping bag between her boots once more while she undid her packet of papers and spread them out on the desk to sort through.

When the duty larval returned she glanced at and selected those of the girl's papers she needed, first turning each one round to face her before sliding them down to her side of the desk. With her spectacles now in place over her tiny black eyes she began to copy out the relevant details onto the forms she'd laid out in preparation.

The girl leant forward to watch, stretching up on tiptoes to see over the height of the desk. Something intrigued her about the speed and precision with which the larval processed the papers. Something stirred in her.

'I could do some of that. If you like. If it helps.'

'You could.' The larval didn't look up. 'But it would take five times as long, and I'd still need to check it over when you were done. The fee is the same either way.'

One of the documents was a photographic passbook, a simple palm-sized fold of debossed black card with fraying corners. The girl had left it closed. Now the larval reached up a small grey hand and slid the item fractionally towards her. She flipped it open. She peered at the picture, then up at the applicant. She closed the book and continued with her form-filling.

The girl laughed nervously.

'You can't possibly tell it's me! Not from that. I have further proof if you need it.'

The clerk glanced up again and smiled.

'It's just a matter of experience. You may not see the similarities. I do. First name?'

The girl paused, frowning.

'Megan. I'm sure it should say in the—'

The clerk shook her head. 'New first name?'

'Oh. I hadn't—must I change?'

The clerk tightened her small grey mouth.

'You can hardly remain a Megan, of all names. Far too larval. Might just as well be a Greta, or worse a full-on Maggie. You really should have thought about this before coming in.'

The girl straightened. She was taller than the clerk, but not by much.

'I didn't think it would matter. Not right away, I mean.' She wrinkled her nose in indecision. 'Is there maybe some sort of list I could choose from?'

'No. It would be interminable, and as such quite use-less. Just so long as you don't go calling yourself Imogen you can pick whatever you like. We get far too many Imogens. I'm sure they all regret it eventually.' She smiled thinly. 'Don't worry though. You can make the alteration later if you so wish. Anyone can. More work for the likes of us and a further fee from yourself. So, all in all, I'd say it's better to pick something presently. I find it hard to believe you haven't thought about this at some point. Everybody knows about it.'

'Oh. I did. Yes. Of course. It's just—I hadn't quite settled. I had thought something like Mabel might be a possibility. Because it's not *so* very different. Then again, if it's really a matter of—'

She stopped. The old larval was staring at her.

It was hard to determine a precise expression from those sharp black eyes, with or without spectacles. She might have been considering the name with all the care and attention that her years of so-called experience had granted her. Or she may simply have been waiting for a better suggestion.

At length the clerk gave an offhand nod.

'Mabel is fine. Nothing wrong with Mabel. Yes. I'll put it in the box.'

The girl leant forward again, straining to see the new name being entered.

The larval continued dispassionately.

'I know what you're thinking. What does this old fool know? What does she even care? But I've been around a good many years, dear. And will be for a good many more. Some of us aren't quite so hasty about these things. Yes, I saw your dates. But for some of us the long wait isn't a drawback. Not by any means. It's an important part of the cycle. And it too has its benefits. More care can be taken. More security. An altogether safer transition.'

The girl laughed.

'You can't make such a change at your age! Surely. It'd be too dangerous.'

The old larval straightened. She lifted two of the documents to the desk top and spun them about to face the girl.

'No more or less a danger than it was for yourself. Just different. And even that can be minimised with the proper care. Regular testing and the like. Not everything has to be rushed into, you know. The body remembers. The body waits.'

She pointed to two large empty boxes at the base of each form.

'When you're ready. Here. And again here. Press firmly.'

She slid a wad of scrap paper towards the girl and laid a pen on top of it.

'You'll want to practice first. Take as long as you like. But not too long. Call me when you're ready and I'll bring the camera through.'

'Oh—you'll do that here as well? Yourself?'

The clerk ignored the implications of the question.

'In any case you've no need to fuss over your appearance. You're fine as you are. And the print is instant, so while it dries I'll have the laminator warmed up and ready to go. After which—that'll be you done.'

The girl stared.

'You mean that's it?'

The larval nodded.

'Apart from payment. Yes. That's it.'

'Oh, payment. Right. Of course.' The girl took a brown envelope from her inside jacket pocket and placed it on the counter. 'It should be the exact figure. I checked it three times over.'

The clerk slipped out the notes, fanned the edges briefly between her fingers, before sliding them back into the envelope. She gave a short smile, letting her black gums show, then headed on through to the back room.

'I'll get a receipt sorted out. Call when you're done.'

The girl opened her mouth to reply but promptly shut it again, turning her attention instead to the wad of scrap paper, upon which she began now to practice a new signature.

Sal's workday was finishing. As he tidied his cubicle, putting all his papers in their right place in preparation for the morning, he saw his movements echoed in the shadows that fell upon the white membrane of his cubicle wall.

He had met his new colleague only briefly. She had been quiet when she arrived, exchanging only a few words of introduction when prompted to do so by the supervisor. Sal hadn't spoken to her since. They both got on with their work separately, diligently. They didn't spend their lunch hours in each other's company. They didn't say goodbye when the time came for them each to go home.

On exiting the building Sal dawdled. It didn't matter now if people saw in what direction he went, whether they wondered or not, it made little difference. He walked slowly, his small cold hands deep in the pockets of his coat. He was already a good way from work when he got the feeling he was being followed. He made sure he never looked directly behind him, noting the details of his pursuer only in glimpses, in sounds: their gaudy clothes, their sure and heavy tread.

Then for a moment the footfalls all but disappeared. When Sal strained to listen he could hear them only faintly, as though very far away, yet moving now much more swiftly. A second later, with a quick rush of air and a sudden flurry of thumps and rustling, his pursuer was upon him.

One arm was clamped around his middle, pinning his own arms in place. At the same time a hot clammy hand was cupped tight over his eyes. Sal wondered at that. In the very moment he was grabbed he wondered that his mouth had been left uncovered. He squirmed. But before he could think what to call out there came a voice, whispering with sweet warm breath close to the pinhole of his ear.

'Oh dear, my boy. Oh deary dear indeed! You should have been *much* more careful. You were *far* too easy a thing to catch. And here's me having been out all the long day. And now I'm hungry. Oh so hungry. I could eat anything. Simply anything! With just a little bite, a little chomp through that young and leafy skin, I could drain you of all your juices. Or—just some of them, maybe.'

Sal tried hard to calm himself. He disliked not being able to move his arms. He wanted to struggle, to lash out with all his strength. He could feel the frustration building inside him, ready to explode in a sudden fury, but he managed for now to restrain such an urge. He breathed out.

'Megan?'

There was a short pause.

'Not any more.'

And the hand slid smoothly away. And the arm at last released him.

Sal spun round at once to look at her.

He'd had no idea from those sneaky glances he'd given that it was her following. This person he'd known near all his life and he'd never have guessed. And now she stood, arms bent outwards, palms upraised, a large shopping bag looped over the crook of one elbow.

She turned on the spot for him, then dipped a hand into her pocket and brought out a new passbook. She stepped forward.

The passbook was dark green. It had gilt edges. Flipping it open to show its glossy interior she pointed with the tip of her thumbnail to the name printed beside her picture.

Sal squinted. He straightened.

'Why Mabel?'

She shrugged.

'Why Sal?'

They began walking together.

'Please say you like the clothes, at least.'

'Where did you get them?'

'They're faulty. Reduced. I'll need more. A proper trip sometime. The boots cost the most. But they'll last. So long as I take care of them.'

'Not if they're faulty.'

'The faults are—well, let's just say they're very very small.'

'I knew it was you. Right away. I knew. And you wouldn't eat me. People don't eat other people.'

Mabel grinned, showing Sal her new white teeth.

'I really am very hungry though. Famished. I just have this urge to eat eat eat!'

They walked in silence for a while. Sal preferred it like that. He was happy simply to have her beside him. If he didn't look at her, if he didn't think about the firm tap of her fancy boots or the bustle of her bulky shopping bag, if he didn't think about the smooth forward flow of her, or the size and strength of her, or the strange new scent of her, then he could feel that this was just the same old Megan.

It certainly wasn't Mabel. He didn't know of any Mabel. That was all just pretence. And Sal didn't like people pretending. Sal liked things to be exactly as they were. How they should be.

'They're advertising for a new supervisor.'

Mabel rolled her eyes.

'I'm not in the least surprised. How many new supervisors did we get through in a year?'

'I thought. I just wondered. Now that you're done. If maybe you—'

Mabel laughed suddenly.

Sal didn't look at her. He didn't want to see that wide red mouth, those shining blue eyes.

Her laugh stopped as abruptly as it had started.

'Now wouldn't that be strange! Don't you think? To go, only to come right back? What would they think of me!'

'They wouldn't know. That it was you. They might not notice. I don't see how they could. Only I'd know.'

'What, and then I'd suggest you for promotion, hmm? Oh, I'm not sure about that, Sal. It sounds shifty. Devious. If ever they found out—'

'I wouldn't want that. I didn't mean that. I'm happy just where I am.'

Mabel shot a glance at him. She took a long breath and held it behind tightened lips before releasing it slowly, letting out a low groan as she did so.

'Oh, I don't know, Sal. To go backwards like that. It would seem—it would feel—don't you think I should be moving on? You could too. Maybe you ought to apply. That'd be something. A step forward. There's no reason a larval couldn't take a senior role. You've been there as long as I have. Longer, if you think how I—'

Sal interrupted her.

'It's only a job. You'll need one. You have to start somewhere. And you know the place. The work. You'd be good. They wouldn't know why. You'd just be really good. They'd be impressed. It would be a good start. And you might like it. You'd see it from both sides. You'd sympathise. You'd know how to deal with disruptions. You'd make it all better.'

They were on her street now. Mabel had slowed her step still further. Sal had matched it. There was no need now to hang back or to hide, but Sal chose not to question the change in pace.

Mabel let out another long sigh.

'You're right, Sal. Of course you are. And thank you for thinking of me. It's a good suggestion. It is. And I do have to start somewhere. So—I'll consider it. I will. Promise.'

'I could get you a form. I could get one tomorrow.'

'Thank you, but—better if I make enquiries myself,

don't you think? It'd seem more professional that way. They'd make a note of that—my initial enquiry, what questions I may ask.'

'Yes.' Sal nodded slowly. 'They'd take notes. They'd notice everything. But I could still help. I only want to help.'

'Oh, and you have, Sal. You really have. And look, you've walked me home too. Like a real gentleman. Thank you. I couldn't ask for a better protector.'

They had stopped. They were outside her building. Sal looked both ways down the street. There was no one about. Mabel leaned a little way forward, her face beside Sal's, at mouth level.

It made Sal feel awkward. He wasn't used to this sort of thing. The smell of her was overwhelming. He wanted to shrink away. And yet he didn't want her to think she'd made him feel uncomfortable. He mustn't let her think that. So he kissed her, very simply and quickly on the cheek, and drew back.

Mabel stayed still for a moment, her eyebrows raised. Then she completed the action that had begun with her leaning forward, transferring the handle of the shopping bag from the crook of her elbow to her wrist, as now with her free hand she fished inside the bag and, after a brief rummage, brought out her key with its dangling glow-worm fob. She smiled at Sal as she held it up.

Sal opened his mouth to speak, forming empty shapes with his lips as he struggled to choose a word to say first.

Mabel glanced behind towards the building, then back at him. She smiled again.

'It's okay. I don't mind. It was very sweet of you. But I need to go in. You'll come by in a few days maybe, yes?'

Sal nodded stiffly. He didn't want to stay in any case. Without further spectacle he turned and walked away.

Mabel giggled softly to herself as she trotted up the stairwell. By the time she'd reached her floor the giggles had subsided into smiles, and as she closed the apartment door behind her she merely shook her head.

She turned instinctively to put the four locks across that Sal had fitted, pausing momentarily with the last between her fingers, examining the crudely-hammered nails of its housing before sighing and sliding the end of the chain into place.

Then she went to the sofa, cleared it of its ugly cushions and, very carefully, piece by piece, took out each new item of clothing from her shopping bag: the delicate silks and brushed cottons in their softly shimmering colours—copper, berry, seashell, leaf. Smiling to herself she unfolded them all, in turn, laying each out flat, and kneeling down she touched them, stroking them with outstretched fingertips.

•

It was in the darkest part of the night when Sal found himself again in the long narrow hallway.

He drew his key glinting from his pocket. It had its own icy light. A pure silvery brightness. It blurred in the hazy thickness of the air. It chimed quietly as he fed it down the fine black grooves of the keyhole.

As slowly he pushed the door open so the chains caught. All four of them catching at once. But Sal kept pushing. And with that gentle obstinacy the yellow links softened, stretching like warm toffee, falling away in sticky filaments.

The girl in the bed hadn't woken. Sal could see the covers rise and fall with her slow deep breathing. The room moved with her, each breath adding to the pressures of the air, bending the walls outward, drawing them in.

Sal peeled the sheets from her. She was naked beneath them, lying curled upon her side. In the thin white light of night her skin looked colourless. It looked grey, like Sal's. He gathered her up from the bed. She was floppy in his arms, her head lolling against his shoulder. A ghostly ragdoll. A dead weight.

The wardrobe was already open. A breeze blew through it, parting the pale hanging veils as Sal carried the sleeping figure through and into the hotness, the moistness, the sizzling darkness of the hidden room.

The couch had dried. Sal laid the girl's length out on the soft grey skin of her chrysalis. He positioned her carefully. He matched each part of her to the skin's imprinted part of her. Then he rolled her up into that casing, pinch-sealing her back inside; her tangle of limbs and bowed sleepy head all balled up tight, with only the bumps of elbows and knees pushing awkwardly against the taut outer film.

But soon those bumps softened, soon they smoothed over, as slowly the girl began to dissolve back into herself. And all the while Sal watched from the opposite corner of the couch; his knees drawn up to his chest, his head bowed forward.

Mabel stood patiently at reception, her boots neatly together, her hands in her jacket pockets. She waited while the duty larval droned quietly into the telephone, his head down, the end of his pen following the narrow column of an open ledger. He hadn't looked up when Mabel approached his desk.

As soon as the call ended and the larval raised his head Mabel smiled broadly and took from her pocket the little fold of paper she'd been clutching. She uncrumpled it as she spoke, sliding it forward over the desk.

'Does he work here? He gave me this. He said I could come by. I've not made an appointment. I don't know if that's necessary. I could do so now if it is necessary. Might it be necessary?'

The duty larval peered forward at the paper. He flattened it with his long soft fingers. He made a downward shape with his mouth and shook his head. Then he wrote a floor and door number on a pad, tore off the sheet, and handed it to Mabel.

She took both it and her own note and folded them into her palm.

'As long as he won't mind. He must be very busy. Shall I sign in as well? I've my pass with me. For identification. If you need it.'

She was already reaching for the open visitor's book beside her but the larval shook his head again and pointed his pen towards the staircase. Then, as though to assure the visitor it was all fine, he gave a short but unconvincing smile and returned his attention to the ledger.

Mabel trotted up the stairs, her bootsoles tapping lightly on each step, her fingertips barely touching the blue banister.

∙

Inspector Augustine was examining a small white fragment of shell when Mabel knocked at his already open door. Several glossy monochrome prints were laid out on the desk, each image an enlargement of other previous enlargements; high contrast, hard to identify individually as anything more than spots of deep shadow and bright jagged shapes; it was only in a row that they seemed to present some sort of sequence, and only then to someone aware of the source.

The inspector held the fragment of shell lightly between the fingers of both hands. He turned it without looking at it. He tested its flexibility in one direction, then the other. The dry fragment bent a good way back before it snapped. A fine pink membrane now held the two pieces together. Augustine tore the membrane and placed both fragments on the desk top, crushing one of them slowly beneath the rounded heel of his fountain pen till all that remained of the shell was coarse white powder, though the pink membrane that had supported it stayed mostly intact.

At Mabel's knock Augustine hastily brushed the powder onto the carpet and stood up straight.

Mabel took a step forward into the room.

'The receptionist said I could come straight up. Or—he suggested I could. I think. Perhaps he phoned you? I don't mind making an appointment if you'd—'

'No, no. Not necessary. Not at all.'

In one smooth gesture Augustine gathered up the photographs, tapping their edges absentmindedly against his palm.

'I'm not doing anything, I've merely been—'

He glanced at the clock and simultaneously laid the photographs face down on his desk.

'Let's go for lunch. Would that be alright? It's not too early. We might just beat the horde.'

So saying he caught up his coat and coming forward ushered Mabel back out of his office and into the corridor, his hand resting lightly against the small of her back. She didn't protest.

•

The eatery they chose was only a short walk along from the inspector's office building. It was a cramped oily-aired sort of place, with a patched linoleum floor and a dozen or so thin-legged tables. Mabel took a seat by the window while Augustine leant up at the front counter, ordering, chatting to whoever was taking his order, and every so often glancing back at Mabel, flashing smiles, rolling his eyes.

The inspector looked very much at ease in such an environment. Mabel guessed that this was likely somewhere he frequented, that these would be people he was familiar with, and they with him.

Mabel was not at ease. All the other people in the eatery were larvals: the other diners, the servers at the hatch, the cooks in the steamy slippery kitchen beyond. For Mabel it should have felt no different from when she'd visited similar places before, except that this time she was herself different. Now she was the oddity, the one out of place, with everything else around her seeming strange. And yet, had she still been a larval, among other larvals, and had there been an adult or two, would she have minded? She didn't believe so. At least she couldn't recall having minded, couldn't transpose her present feelings into that old situation.

Sitting by the window proved to be a regrettable decision. With everyone that passed, even if they didn't look in directly, Mabel felt they could see her, that they were aware of her, of her exposure, and that they were indeed wondering about her, questioning her appearance, her mere presence in such a place. It made her anxious. It made her feel like an impostor. It made her want to get out of the eatery, either right away or as soon as would be deemed appropriate.

Augustine came over with their tray of food. He slid Mabel's share of plates and cups and napkin-rolled cutlery towards her. She dug in at once. A thick-cut grilled steak sandwich with fried egg and cheese, plus a side plate crudely piled with glistening chips.

Mabel bit deeply into the sandwich, holding it with both hands. The inspector picked at his chips, watching Mabel closely.

'Not perhaps for me to say, but you probably shouldn't gobble your food like that. I mean, it's not like anyone will mind, but the action doesn't exactly fit the image.'

Mabel put her hand in front of her full mouth.

'Didn't you?' She had to chew a bit more before continuing. 'When you first emerged? When you came out and found you had teeth? Real teeth? Didn't you want to use them? To gorge? You must have been hungry. I've been ever so hungry.'

'For a while. I suppose. Yes.' The inspector shrugged. 'But only a while. You need to stay in control of your body. Not the other way around. If you're hungry then it's telling you something. But you'll know all about that, I'm sure. Who was it helped you, by the way?'

'I was given a pamphlet. It was very useful.'

'A pamphlet! Right, of course—and no bad thing.' The inspector laughed and shook his head. 'I do sometimes wonder though. All the centres we've set up, just for this sort of thing. The free advice. The offers of care, of safety. And still people settle for the squalid little flat, far away from anywhere, and no more than a crumpled pamphlet to see them through. Not that I'm knocking the pamphlets. After all if it wasn't for those—'

He spread his hands.

'Oh, I know.' Mabel grinned, her mouth full once again. 'And I did get through.'

'True. Very true.' The inspector nodded. He ate another chip. 'And now? How is Sal dealing with it? How does he feel about you?'

'We have a link.' Mabel swallowed hard. She took a sip of coffee, winced at the bitterness, and began afresh. 'We've known each other so long, you see. I couldn't have got through it without him. Or—maybe I could. I don't know. But I'm glad he was there. I didn't know it, of course. I mean, I don't think so. And yet I think—I think I did sort of know it. That he was there. All the time that I—wasn't.'

'And what about when you go away? You think he'd follow? Is Sal someone to be led by your example?'

'Oh, I'm not going away. That's exactly what I mean. I wouldn't desert him. Not ever. I want to help, see? That's what I've been thinking I'll do. I want to spread awareness. To educate. To be involved. As you are.'

'Oh, you really wouldn't want that. Trust me. Not what I do.'

'No, well—I don't actually know what you do. I just mean to help people through it. To show that it's okay—on the other side. Like you said, to act as an example, maybe.'

'And you can. You could.' Augustine nodded slowly. He took a long slow breath. 'It's a worthwhile endeavour. And in some ways I approve. I do. Really. But you'd need a proper job as well. And you'd need to do that job for a while before you take on a second role. You know, to get a bit of experience.'

'I thought you said there were centres, that there were

people who provide this sort of support, this very thing. That's a job, isn't it?'

'Oh, indeed. I even know someone that runs one. A centre, that is. I could put you in contact. Arrange matters. No trouble. But none of it pays well. Not well at all. And then where would you be? What sort of example? What incentive? It really is much better if you do this kind of thing in your spare time. It looks better that way too. And then have that proper job, that well-paid job, to keep you going. You could get one now. Easily. Now that you're—as you are. I can help you with that. I can help you with both this and that.'

Mabel frowned, thinking hard.

'And Sal?'

'I've always looked after Sal. As much as I'm able. Don't you worry about him. He's not the issue presently. He's stable. He's secure. What's important is you push forward. Continue what you've started. Get away for a while. Put to use what you've gained. Not stick around here. Not right now. Try the south, perhaps. I can easily fix up a job for you. Just like that.' He snapped his fingers. 'Good character references. Contacts. And you've money for a place to live, yes?'

'Of course. I saved up. For years. This wasn't a spur-of-the-moment thing. Not even Sal knew. He wouldn't have approved.'

'And this too will help him. It'll help him see that everyone else around him is getting on. That he'll be left behind if he doesn't—well, make the effort.'

'Yes. I can see that.' Mabel slouched in her seat, her

coffee cup between both hands, her lips pursed. 'Yes. I guess that does make sense.'

Augustine shrugged. 'And all you really need to do right now is go and put things in order for leaving. You're already in the best mode for this. Keep that momentum going. I'll fix the rest. Think of it as something for Sal. And for yourself, of course. Mainly for yourself. It should only take a day to sort, at most. Perhaps mere hours if you're lucky. Depends. But the sooner the better, no?'

Mabel nodded.

They sat in silence for a while, the inspector still picking at his food, Mabel watching him.

At length she pointed.

'If you're not going to finish that—it really would be a shame.'

The plate was duly slid in her direction.

It was near closing time in the department store. Sal had hurried there straight after work.

At the end of the aisle in which he now loitered was a large convex mirror. He appeared very small in it. One of the larval storekeepers had been keeping an eye on him since he arrived, though they'd not followed him to this particular area at the very back of the store. If they could indeed see him in the mirror he doubted they'd be able to see much of what he may or may not be doing.

But Sal didn't like being watched. It made him feel as though he was the sort of person who needed to be watched, the sort of person who looked like he might take something. It prompted him to consider the option. It made him think how easy it would be.

He didn't know what the scarf he was examining was made from. It didn't say silk anywhere on the box. It was as thin and as light as Sal thought silk ought to be, though not quite as smooth and soft as the panties he'd accidentally stolen, the ones Megan had made such a fuss over.

The scarf was green and yellow. The colours were vivid. Unevenly patched. They overlapped and bled into one another so that if Sal held the misty fabric loosely, at arm's length, and squinted at it, and moved his head from side to side, it gave the vague impression of sunlight shining through treetops.

The scarf, whatever it was made from, was expensive, even after its sale discount. Opened out it was as long as it was wide. This amounted to a lot of material. And yet the scarf packed up tightly and was designed to come in a thin aluminium tube with a screw cap. The wearer could then, so the advertisement stated, pour it out like a liquid to settle around one's shoulders. Sal thought the scarf would more than likely get stuck in its tube, but he added the item to his basket nonetheless, along with the tinned roe and the little tub of pâté he'd already selected from other aisles.

He glanced up at the mirror. No one appeared to be watching. Not just then. That area of the store seemed now to be empty but for himself. With a few things in his basket, those he fully intended to pay for, he could easily slip another item into his pocket, if he so wished. Something small. That'd be the best way to do it, if indeed he was going to do it. They'd never suspect that.

He made his way to the checkout.

•

Sal hesitated in Mabel's hallway before knocking. He could hear movement from within. A muffle of footfalls. Soft thumps. The radio was on. He lifted his hand but the sound of another door opening made him stop.

The noise had come from behind him. He turned to look but all the doors on the hallway's opposite side appeared closed, at least from the angle at which he could see them.

Sal knocked. He heard as the radio was turned off. He saw the pale pin of the peephole briefly darken. There was a pause. Then more footfalls, scufflings, thumps. At length the chains were undone and Mabel opened up to let him in.

'You only just caught me. I'm not long back myself.'

Mabel went at once to slump on the sofa. She patted the seat beside her for Sal to sit too. His eyes travelled quickly round the room as he crossed towards her.

The wardrobe door was open, a couple of plastic hangers lay on the floor. On the bed were neat piles of clothes, new and old, arranged by type. The bed itself was unaccountably lumpy: two large square mounds, covered by the bedsheets.

Sal pretended he hadn't seen. He sat staring at the floor as Mabel spoke.

'I'm afraid I can't be long, Sal. I've something important to be getting on with this evening. I hope you don't mind. It's very nice to see you. Would you like something to eat? I could make you a mash. Are you thirsty?'

Sal drew a small parcel from the inside pocket of his old anorak. He gave it to Mabel. She took it delicately, her eyes glinting, biting her lower lip to stop from smiling. As she unwrapped the tissue paper she glanced upward, but Sal's face was unreadable.

The cold silvery tube was of the same width as her thumb. She frowned at it for a moment before twisting off the cap and looking inside. She didn't pour out its contents. Instead she reached in with her fingertips and pulled at a protruding fold of yellow-green fabric.

The scarf came out with a soft hiss, half-expanding half-flopping to the sofa.

Mabel pinched two corners and held her arms wide, the scarf hanging as a veil between Sal and herself, its many sharp creases offset by the interplay of colours. She let it crumple again to her lap and leaning forward kissed Sal on the cheek. He didn't move.

'I hope it wasn't expensive. It looks quite expensive. Is it silk? It doesn't matter if it's not silk. But silk is so so expensive.'

From the outer pockets of his coat Sal now took three further tissue-wrapped items. These he placed upon the table.

Mabel was about to speak, to say she couldn't possibly accept so many gifts, but Sal had seen something. On the table, beside the little parcels he'd just set down, were two cardboard tags, each with plastic ties sticking out, the ends of which had been cut. Sal picked up one of the tags. On it was the picture of a suitcase. Sal looked at the picture, then over at the bed, at the two square lumps under the bedclothes. Mabel swallowed.

'It's only a preparation. Nothing has been planned, but I really wanted to get this place in order. And of course I can't stay here indefinitely. It's not a very nice area. But you know that, right? And anyway a lot of the clothes in the wardrobe were just to fill out the space. It was about time I sorted through things.'

Sal nodded. He stood up.

Mabel remained seated. She watched Sal make his way to the door.

'What about these other presents? Don't you want to see me open those as well?' She picked up the smallest and put it to her nose. 'Oh, this one smells lovely! Won't you stay a while longer?'

The door was already open. Sal looked back briefly and shook his head, before stepping out and closing the door behind him.

In the hallway Sal made a conscious effort to tread very quietly as he moved away. Upon turning onto the stairwell he heard once again the sound of a door opening. He stopped and waited. A few moments later the door was closed. He waited for the sounds of the chains being put across but didn't hear them.

He sat down upon the polished concrete steps and listened. It would take her a moment to open the parcels. It would take her a little more time to think about what to do next. She would guess he wouldn't walk fast. She would know what direction he'd be headed in. She could run much faster than he could, if she wanted.

Sal strained his ears for any little sound. There was a metallic tapping and a sort of low persistent hum, but that might just have been the building itself. He listened for the quiet garble of the radio being turned back on but it never came.

Even when he did at last stand up and make his way down the stairs Sal moved with deliberate slowness. And once out on the street he dug his hands in his pockets and checked all directions over-thoroughly before scuffing away homewards. It would be strange if Mabel did indeed come after him only to find he'd hardly got to the end of the road, but he didn't worry too much about that. Her coming at all would be enough.

An approaching taxi gave him the excuse, before he reached the first turning, to at last look round, watching as the vehicle passed. But there was not the hoped-for figure on the pavement following him.

The taxi slowed.

Sal couldn't be certain from where he stood but it seemed very much as though the taxi stopped just outside Mabel's building. Sal waited, watching. A short while later a figure dashed out from the glass doors and into the taxi.

It had happened in a mere moment but Sal could clearly make out the green and yellow scarf that flapped around the figure's shoulders.

As the taxi moved away Sal began walking back once more towards the building. He checked his pockets and brought out the stout flexible square of misty plastic. He tapped it idly against the fingers of one hand as he slipped back in through the building's glass front doors. Then he stood still.

Someone was standing in the brightly lit entrance hall. It was the same old larval he'd often seen on Mabel's floor. The only other person he'd ever seen in the building, and only then as glimpses through the door. But now she was standing directly in front of him, gazing right at him, wearing a curious smile that might have been sympathetic, or might have been something else.

The restaurant had, at first glance, seemed more Mabel's sort of place. Other than the larval waiters the only people dining there were adults like herself. She had felt more comfortable from the start. Even the few looks she'd received upon entering and taking her seat had pleased her. These looks had been from men. They continued throughout the meal, surreptitious turns of the head whenever she moved, as though those around her couldn't help but look her way. She pretended not to notice. A suppressed smile was all the signal she returned.

'Well, it's there if you want it. All set. You just have to accept. It's nothing too special. Not just yet. But a job is a job, right? Something to start you off with.'

The inspector too had rarely let his eyes fall from her, even while he ate. He seemed to have very little awareness of those around them. But this was of course mere politeness on his part, and it pleased Mabel to have someone focus on her so attentively.

'And if you don't like it it doesn't matter. Something else can be found. Easy. But this will at least get you going. And my friend knows the situation. She'll be very understanding. Not everyone is.'

Augustine had noticed her scarf at once. He had commented upon it, how well it suited her other colours. She still had on the same outfit she'd worn when first he met her. The same striped lilac and mauve jacket. The yellow skirt. The fine blue blouse. Or no, perhaps the blouse had been a different colour. Augustine wasn't sure he could remember. He felt tired from the day's work. His mind felt fuzzy. Still he kept talking to her. It was easy to direct all his thought towards her. And the scarf settled around her shoulders more like a shawl. A yellow-green haze. Her bright face floating above it. And the pinkening in her golden hair. Though perhaps that was the lighting? No, of course, he was wrong, he now realised, totally wrong! When first he'd met her she hadn't been wearing these clothes at all. She'd been wrapped in a towel and an old baggy shirt. And her hair, and the rest of her too, had been sopping wet.

'Even if eventually you wish to return here. To this town, I mean. I could understand that. That's understandable. Yes. Truly. It's just as much a possibility as anything else. At least you'll have tried. At least you can't say you haven't explored further afield.'

He had given her the ticket after their first course. He had taken it coolly from his pocket and slid it forward over the glossy tablecloth. Now it nestled between her side plate and her cream-smeared pudding bowl. He had meant it when he said he didn't mind if she never used it, that it had no set expiry, that all it did was provide her with an option, taking away one further strand of decision-making. All she needed to do was hop on the train if and when she felt ready to do so. But he could see she was pleased with it. Aside from the occasional glances around the room, and her looking long at him, he could see her eyes flick to it now and again, as though suddenly reminded of its presence, or else to assure herself it was really there.

'And with her connection to the education centres, really it's the perfect opportunity for you. Not just a mentor, a good friend. You'll like her. I'm sure of that. She's like you. Older, but like you. I've known her a long time. Yes, a long long time. And if you don't get on? Well, these things happen. It's nothing to be concerned about. You can call me again. We can find something else.'

Now that the meal was finished Mabel was sitting forward in her seat, her elbows on the table and shoulders slightly tensed as with both hands she cradled her tumbler of water, as though with her whole body she wished to protect it, taking from it regular little sips, not wanting for it ever to be empty.

Only when another diner sneezed, a man a few tables away, did Mabel turn her head sharply to look at him. And as he pulled a handkerchief from his pocket to dab at his nose so his eyes angled oddly towards her, as though she was herself partly to blame for his sudden outburst.

The lady this man was with also turned to look. Where the man's expression had been one of curious concern the lady's seemed somehow disapproving. And as Mabel turned back to Augustine, who appeared not to have noticed any such disturbance, several other heads also turned back to their meals, some of them pinching or rubbing at their noses.

'I don't know when I last saw her. No. Can't altogether be sure on that. She moved away, you see. A long long time ago.

But I do trust her. She's that sort of person. She has that sort of aura. I can't explain it any other way.'

Mabel found this new attention a delightful curiosity. It was only present in other adults. Perhaps they were somehow aware of her general newness. Perhaps they felt protective of her, wanting to help, just as Augustine seemed eager to help.

It was not like that with the larvals. Her taxi driver had been perfectly civil with her, yes, but he'd not shared her excitement about the expensive restaurant he was to be taking her to. For him she was merely a fare. He clearly didn't understand good eating. The larval waiter, too, barely looked at her. His politeness and gentle servitude was addressed mainly towards the inspector. Mabel didn't mind that one bit. It was the inspector after all who would be paying for the meal. And perhaps these two were familiar. Perhaps the inspector came to this restaurant fairly regularly. Perhaps with other young adults like herself. Perhaps he liked helping people in her situation. No, she didn't at all mind this idea. It only endeared him to her further. It made her feel still more willing to accept his kind offers of help.

'Because that does happen, of course. People do move away. They go to other towns. Other countries. They explore. And maybe they come back. Or maybe they never go away. That's also a choice that can be made. There's nothing wrong with that. There's important work to be done. Always. Everywhere. So very important.'

Another sneeze. The same man as before. But this time, at the sudden blast of that sneeze, two other men at neighbouring tables stood up abruptly. Their attentions, however, were not directed towards the sneezer. They were both looking at Mabel.

One was at a table close to her own. As he sat slowly down again it was possible to see his nose twitching, the nostrils flaring. The impression might have been of frustration, even anger, were it not for his eyes, which were soft, concerned, almost pleading. Till the woman he was with regained his attention. Though when she too glanced over her shoulder at Mabel there was a definite air of hostility in her look. A pursing of lips. A tightening of the jaw.

'So there are good reasons. Yes. Can't deny that. Both to go and to stay. People do need to be looked after. Watched over. There's always time. Plenty. Years and years. But if there's nothing holding you back right away. No good reason to stay, I mean. Then again if there's no good reason to go—'

Mabel reached over and laid her hand gently on Augustine's arm.

He stopped talking at once. He stared at her hand upon his sleeve. He stared but he didn't move. As though he didn't want to move. He just wanted to see what that hand and that touch might choose to do next.

Only when Mabel started whispering did he look up at her, though she did not take her hand from his arm.

'I think we ought to go now. I mean from here. I mean leave the restaurant. But please, don't stop telling me whatever it is you're telling me. I think we should just do so somewhere quieter. Somewhere—where others are not.'

She was very calm. The environment around her was certainly a strange one even though she did not herself feel especially perturbed. She was getting well used to this new way of being.

The inspector swayed a little as he stood up. He rustled some notes from his wallet to the table. He didn't count them. He was sure they would cover whatever expense the meal had incurred.

Mabel raised her eyebrows at this dismissive manner but she didn't question it. And as they both left the restaurant she was aware of seats sliding back and of other diners half-getting to their feet.

But once outside, when she and the inspector walked back past the restaurant, and Mabel glanced in through the small round windows, she saw that everyone was still seated, chatting and eating contentedly. There had been no apparent disturbance. Nothing for anyone to be concerned about.

·

The inspector's own apartment was small, situated below street level, but well-heated. After the freshness of their slow walk through town Mabel was glad of the sudden warmth. Her cheeks were soon flushed and she took off her scarf, laying it neatly over the back of an armchair. But since the flimsy garment had itself provided very little warmth it was soon followed by her striped jacket, which she folded lengthways and laid carefully over the scarf.

Augustine continued to talk as he pottered about, moving from one room to another and back out again with the air of someone who has half-forgotten what he went into such rooms to do.

'And if one town doesn't suit you, well then, try another. Or your job, or your life, or your friends. It's a big enough world. It's only important that you're happy in it. I mean, really happy. And that you can make others happy too. But you'll be hungry now, yes? Or maybe you're thirsty. Are you hungry? I could make you something. I've plenty in the cupboards.'

'Actually, you know what, I feel quite full up.' Mabel pressed her palm to her belly, feeling the pressure there, the push of her insides. 'A little bloated even. I thought our walk might do me some good. That is, to help things go down? Thank you, though. It's very kind of you. But I doubt I'll need to eat anything more for a week!'

Augustine surveyed her with concern.

'Do you feel alright? Are you tired? You can have a nap if you like. I won't mind. My place is—you know. Yes. Whatever you feel like. Just do.'

'Oh—no. Thank you. I'm not tired in the slightest. I didn't mean that exactly. I've enough energy to talk all night. If you wanted to talk, I mean. And the walk was perfect. I simply—couldn't eat another thing.'

'And to drink?'

'Water is just fine, thank you. Nice cool water.'

Augustine brought her a glass, having left the kettle hissing in his kitchen. He'd made nothing for himself. He gave Mabel the glass and stood watching her hold it, her two hands clasped about it, just as she'd done in the restaurant. She was sitting forward, her shoulders hunched, the glass held close to her chest, protectively.

Then Augustine realised he was staring, and with a sharp intake of breath and a quick shake of the head he moved away again, back into the kitchen to deal with the protestations and hissing alarms of the kettle.

Mabel looked around at the small room, its busy walls of bookshelves and mismatched cupboards. The smallness of the space surprised her. But she didn't mind it. It didn't feel so very cramped. It felt just right.

'I like it in here. It's a nice space. Very—homely. Cosy even. And there's a nice—' She paused to think. 'Smell. I don't know whether it's the books or whathaveyou, but it's—nice.'

'I've never really thought about it. I suppose you don't notice such things in your own home. But you're probably right.'

He stood carelessly in the doorway behind her, leaning against the jamb, breathing slowly in through his nose.

'Yes. I do see what you mean. Ha! You'd think I'd have noticed it when we came in. But no, or rather—yes, there it is!'

He went back into the kitchen and stared at the now-quiet kettle. Then he stared at the cup he'd already placed out beside it. He didn't seem to understand what such objects were doing there, or what indeed he might now do with them. He went to put the cup back in the cupboard. Then he decided better of it and left it where it was. He wandered back to the front room.

Mabel hadn't adjusted her position in the slightest. She seemed quite fixed in her shape, though her eyes followed the inspector's motions as he moved round to, then slumped down in, the seat opposite hers.

She tipped her head to one side.

'You've not taken off your coat. Aren't you hot?'

Augustine examined the item in question, lifting a corner of the supple leather as though he was surprised he owned such a costly garment. He laughed loudly. Unnecessarily so. Mabel's eyes widened, though the laughter stopped as abruptly as it had begun.

'You're quite right.'

The inspector stood up, seemingly too fast, for he swooned a little, and then, gripping the arms of the chair, very gently and precisely lowered himself down again. He placed his head in his hands and pressed his fingers into his face, rubbing at the skin as he drew his hands away.

Mabel was smiling. She felt very slightly giddy, but no less alert and eye-bright. It was intriguing watching Augustine, watching him struggle to his feet again and move towards the window. With the apartment being below ground level the windows were mere strips of reinforced and stippled glass set high on the wall, close to the low ceiling. Augustine had to stretch over the top of a deep-set bookshelf in order to undo the catches. But having his arms above his head proved too much for him. Failing to get fresh air into the room he gave up, letting his arms flop. He turned about, steadying himself against the shelves as he did so.

'Wait. I think—I think I know this.' His voice was slurred. He winced with the effort of thinking. He had to swallow several times, tightening his jaw in an effort to retain control. 'I remember now—what this is. I should know. I—should have known. I—'

He managed at last to shrug his heavy coat from his shoulders, leaving it where it fell, bunched into a thick ring round his feet. The drop in temperature this action provided him with was small, its effects short-lived.

He pressed the heels of his palms into his eyes.

'It's—not your fault. I know—I know what you're doing. I should have—I never should have. This isn't— yes. You need to—no. I need to—'

He sank to the floor.

Pulling his knees to his chest he put his arms around them, hugging them tightly. Then, with his head down, he began to moan. Very quietly at first, though the noise grew, slowly, and held. A low pulsating hum.

And Mabel sat on the edge of her chair with her cheeks flushed, smiling, staring wide-eyed at the inspector.

She clutched her glass of water. She sipped from it now and again. She listened to the humming. She wondered at the depth of its note, its penetrative tone. And she waited, eager to see what might happen when the humming stopped.

The old larval shuffled on ahead of Sal. She walked with a stoop, her body bending forward at the chest, all her attention focussed on the placing of her feet.

She didn't have to look behind to check on whether or not the boy followed, she expected him to without special encouragement. She moved very cautiously up the stairs, making sure both feet were planted steadily on any one step before proceeding to the next.

She muttered as she went. It was easy for Sal to hear her so long as he didn't hang back too far; the quietness of her voice resounding clearly within the bare stone walls of the stairwell.

'Oh yes, I know well enough what you've been up to! You and that girl. Yes. I'm not so daft. I know what the likes of her come here for. And I did wonder, at first, oh yes, when I saw you, if maybe you weren't to be trusted. But I had my eye on you! Strange boy that you are. I started to wonder perhaps you were going to go the same way. Now that really would have been something. Oh indeed. Quite irregular! But I see now you're of a different sort. A more thoughtful sort. Cautious. Yes. That's exactly what you are!'

It wasn't that Sal was reluctant to follow. He knew he didn't have to. He could leave at any moment, simply turn and walk away. The old larval probably wouldn't even notice him go. She probably half-expected it. But if she knew something about Mabel's intentions, if she could help in some small way, it would do no harm to go with her for the time being. And he knew how to keep his distance, if required.

Her door was at the far end of the hallway; she went in ahead, leaving it open for him to follow. It was only slightly less dim through the door than out in the hallway itself. And Sal could still hear the old larval muttering, even now she was out of sight.

'You should have knocked. Yes indeed. While you were there. While in residence, as it were. You could have. Day or night. Oh no, I'd not have minded! I knocked on your door. I did, that's right. Just the once. Did you hear me? I thought you were inside. But maybe that wasn't you. No? It doesn't matter. But I thought it better not to knock any more. Not if you weren't going to answer! And it was quite up to you what you did. Oh yes, it's always and precisely up to you.'

Once inside Sal found another hallway, this one running parallel to the main hallway and seemingly as long. Except this second hall was thickly carpeted. This hall was clean. Several rooms led off from it. It was clear now to Sal that all the apartments on this side of the floor had been merged, the inner walls reordered, rebuilt.

The door as he closed it behind him was notably heavy. It had two separate mortise locks. Both sprang into place at the press of a button, clunking deep into the supporting wall. Much more secure than the locks Sal had fitted. His trick with the bit of plastic certainly wouldn't have worked on these.

All those other doorways he had seen from the outer hallway must be false. Inside he could find no trace of them. All boarded up and thickly wallpapered. He couldn't even see an outline.

'Oh yes, I know a lot of things. All sorts of things. I know who actually owns the flat over the way. That's right. I don't see them, but I *know* them. And I know full well what it's rented out for. Oh yes! I've seen enough come and go over the years. I keep my eye on things. You might even call me the landlady. I get paid for it too! Only a little, mind you. But it all adds up. I don't even have to do much. What could I do? An old larval like me! But if something happens, well, then I'm here to raise the alarm. There's a number I'm to call. I know it by heart.'

Framed paintings hung at regular intervals on the hallway walls. Sal couldn't make out the pictures themselves, they were just splodges of bright colour and overlapping shapes, but they intrigued him. He touched first one and then another as he passed. They each felt warm.

He followed the old larval's voice to the end of the hallway, stepping into a space that on its own could have held twice that which Mabel's rooms had occupied.

'They come, they go quiet for a time, and then they leave. And not quite in the same manner that they arrived. No indeed! That is, at least, some do. Some make it through. And all the while I stay put. I'm right here. There's no rushing these things. I've been saving up! Oh yes. Very slowly. Very surely. Perhaps I'll fade away before I ever put my savings to use. Maybe. Possibly. I can't tell for certain. Who can? I don't suppose it really matters either way. Oh no. Not really.'

The first thing to catch Sal's attention on entering the room was a large television set. It was much larger than the set Madox had. It took up one whole corner of the room. It wasn't presently switched on but its cabinet doors were wide open, with the bulge of its huge square eye left grossly protruding.

Even in such a big space the television set was imposing. Nothing in the room could escape that dead-eyed glare. Sal could see the diminished movements of his own dark reflection, squirming somewhere deep beneath its glassy sheen, its faultless grey-black lens.

'I've taken a good few hatchlings in myself. In my time. Oh yes. That pays a little too! I always apply for whatever I'm entitled to. You must. It all adds up. And the more the better. Don't you think? They've all gone now. All my children. Only me remaining. But there will be others. Oh yes. Always others. They always come. My last was a girl. Oh, my daughter! I looked after her as well as ever I might. That's right. Just as someone must have looked after you. Yes? Everyone needs looking after. Even adults. They do! Though they wouldn't dare admit it.'

The old larval came out from an adjoining room, carrying a tray. She approached Sal.

With just a nod she bade him sit, and Sal sat. The tray was placed before him: a large dish of thick green soup and a bowl of fresh potato salad.

The soup was hot. She wouldn't have had time to make it since he'd arrived. Sal wondered then if she'd meant to eat it herself, but he didn't ask, and he didn't complain.

'Then one day she ups and goes! My last daughter, this is. One day she just disappears. Couldn't even trust her old mother. And who knows where she is now. Or if she is! But I can't regret looking after her those many years. Oh no. Raising her from just a little creature, fresh out of its egg. It's true. Just as you yourself were! Oh yes. You must have been. And I'll bet your own mother doesn't know where you are either. Where you've been hiding all this time. Hmm?'

The old larval didn't sit while Sal ate, she continued to move around, chattering all the while, picking up this, reorganising that, sorting magazines in a magazine rack, putting away the ironing board, carrying neatly folded piles of clothes to other rooms.

Even with all this space, and only her in it, she utilised every corner. She filled the place out with her concentrated presence.

'Oh, I know just what you want. You want to find out where she's got to. Yes? Your friend? You don't want her to go but still you want to know where she's gone! You want to track that taxi. Yes? Phone the company? Play detective? Well, I've a phone here, you know. Oh yes. Or there's a payphone downstairs in the entrance hall, if you want a bit of privacy, that is. Next to the main door? But it won't help you. No. They wouldn't give you the answer you wanted. Even if you claimed it was an emergency. Even if you pleaded!'

Sal needed to pee. The old larval pointed him off down the inner hallway, though she followed behind for a short way, carrying a rubbery pot plant into one of the empty bedrooms.

Sal found the bathroom easily enough. The bath itself was vast: deep and square-sided, with tiny alternating pink and cream tiles, and steps cut into the side. It was far too big for a single person. It would use too much water. It would be wasteful. If need be several larvals could have soaked in there together.

The toilet itself was in a separate small room, beyond the one that housed the giant bath. The room had no door, just a gap.

Sal slid his trousers to his ankles and sat down, unable to go at first for staring at that opening, that simple gap. But the seat was warm and the carpet was soft, springy beneath his shoes, and he could still hear the old larval's voice, distantly, so he managed to relax a little.

He had been desperate, and the loudness of his full stream hitting the water made him tense up, ever so slightly. But the old voice beyond never wavered.

'And you couldn't stop her, in any case. Not now. No indeed. She's getting on with whatever she's getting on with! Unless perhaps you follow her. Go the very same way she went? Though that might take you longer than you'd like. And you don't seem the sort of boy who'd want to do a thing like that. Oh no. You seem far more sensible. Far more of a sticking sort. Cautious! Yes. That's what you are. Waiting till just the right moment, no doubt. Saving up! Just like me. Oh, we'd get on very nicely, you and I. Don't you think? Just being what we are and making the most of that. And all before we have a try at being something else.'

Even when Sal finished and had dabbed himself dry, he lingered for a while more, alone in the bathroom.

He took a long time washing his hands, letting them soak in hot water till they felt like they glowed. The bar of unscented grey soap was very large, uncomfortably square and clearly unused, its indented lettering and rough seam still prominent as he twirled it awkwardly between wet hands.

He could imagine it all without any particular effort. He could see himself waking up here each day. It would always be warm. The towels would be fresh and soft. The food would be good. It was all so very easy. So very convenient.

He would get fat. He would begin to feel safe. He would lower his guard.

'She won't forget you though. You needn't ever worry yourself about that! She'll not forget what you've done. Though she may not think about it very often. Oh, but when she does, when her old life enters her mind, even for a moment, there you'll be! Just as you always were. But you don't need to think that way yourself. Not you. Oh no. You can remember her as often as you like! You can think about the choices she made and what they made of her. How much she changed. What she chose then to forget. But you don't need to forget. Not one bit! You can keep your mind full. Full of all the many things that never deserted you.'

When Sal came out of the bathroom the old larval was in the hallway, at its far end, standing slightly stooped within the open frame of the door that led to the television room. She wasn't talking any more, she was simply watching him.

The main door lay between them. When Sal moved towards it the old larval stayed just where she was. When he undid the locks she merely smiled. She nodded as he stood upon the threshold.

Sal stepped into the coldness of the outer corridor.

27. HAVENS

It was long past midnight. The taxi driver was dozing when the knock came at his window. He startled into sudden wakefulness.

He was used to the shock of this. It took him only moments to adjust. And he was used to the state of his late-night passengers, at this hour they were rarely talkative. It was an easy shift for him. He could deliver his fare, return to the rank, and doze again. The passengers themselves would often snooze all the way. The taxi driver liked this, it made him feel protective towards them. The streets were quiet. He would try to drive gently, rocking them to sleep.

But the girl was a worry. She was quiet in all the wrong ways. She didn't relax and lean back sleepily against the headrest. She sat on the edge of the rear seat, bowed forward. She was near doubled over, her head drooping low, her arms hugging tight to her midriff, holding her striped purple jacket firmly closed.

'You alright, Miss?'

He watched for a response in his mirror. He saw as she lifted her head. A brief upward glance. But she didn't look at him, and she didn't reply. She just moaned a bit and ducked her head back down.

•

Mabel felt more than a little disoriented when she woke. It was to be expected, having found herself lying alone on a small high bed in a cramped and unfamiliar bedroom.

The dizziness soon cleared. Her skirt was rucked above her knees. Mabel tugged at the hem, smoothing the yellow fabric back out. She pulled her soft black stockings up as well, one having wrinkled itself down past her heel.

She couldn't find her panties anywhere. This annoyed her. They were expensive, and of good quality, and she didn't yet have many pairs. But it wasn't just that, they had an importance for her that went beyond mere practicality.

·

In the back of the taxi Mabel allowed herself to moan again. There had been another long sharp pain. The moaning seemed to help.

She couldn't double herself up any more than she already was. She couldn't stretch out on the seat. She couldn't do anything other than clutch herself and moan. It was vaguely soothing, letting the low buzz vibrate deep inside her. And yet the next white jagged flash of pain still came on as strongly as all those before it.

She bit down on her lip as the hurt surged through her. She tensed all her muscles, suppressing the urge to cry out.

When this time the agony subsided Mabel gingerly dipped one hand backward under her skirt, as far as she could reach. She dabbed at something gelatinous, something warm and smooth and tacky to the touch.

Withdrawing and examining her fingers she saw only that something now coated their tips, something that glistened darkly in the slow yellow strobe of the street-lights.

·

Mabel found the main room was just as empty and quiet as the bedroom had been.

There, draped over the back of the armchair, she found her jacket. There too were her long brown boots, lying flopped and unzipped, crumpled by their own weight to the floor.

A light was on in the kitchen. Mabel went to get a drink of water.

She emptied the glass in just a few long glugs. Refilling it to the brim she drank down another measure, then twice more, till at length she felt full, till she felt that press of cool liquid balancing her out, stabilising her.

·

The slowing of the taxi was her first relief. Mabel tried to undo herself from the back seat, unfolding her body with care. With a trembling hand she fished in her pockets for money.

She felt the small black eyes of the driver watching her intently. She heard him offer to help, but she shook her head. Having paid him she got out of the taxi as quickly as she could manage and made for the always-open gap in the glass frontage of her building.

She didn't like that the taxi lingered. She feared the driver would follow her upstairs, under a pretence of worry. She was unable just now to run, but she hobbled as best she could up the stone steps, waiting to hear the rising whine of the engine as the taxi moved away, or else the thunk of a car door and footsteps coming through the entrance hall.

But there was nothing. There was only herself: her blind stumble, her fumble with the key, the yawn of the room as she got the door open, her fingers trying clumsily to fit at least two chains across.

When at length she flopped down on the sofa she began to sob, the jerking contraction of each sob hurting her still more deeply inside.

•

Mabel perched on the hard padded arm of the chair. She was already in her jacket. She took her time now, pulling on and zipping up each soft leather boot.

She glanced around the room, her idle gaze settling on a narrow chest of drawers. She smiled at a sudden idea. If she couldn't find her own underwear she could maybe steal some of his. He could surely afford it. And it wouldn't truly be a theft. More of a swap.

There was a mirror hung above the chest of drawers. As Mabel neared it and saw herself approaching she wondered if perhaps her hair was looking darker than it should. It didn't have quite the same metallic sheen she'd become accustomed to. She put it down to nothing more than the dingy light of the basement flat.

The first drawer she tried contained not clothes but various oddments of stationery: lidless pens and coloured paperclips, all stuck together in one stiff clump by the perished rubber of old elastic bands. Mabel rummaged deeper.

At the back of the drawer she found a passbook. It was made of stiff black card, the edges well worn. She didn't at all recognise the scratched and faded picture of the larval inside. The printed name was Gus. It was a common enough larval name. Mabel turned idly round with the passbook still in her hand.

That was the moment it hit her. The pain was truly horrible. She lost all strength in her legs. She doubled up and buckled forward onto her knees.

•

Even lying on her own familiar couch with her boots kicked off and her stockings unpeeled provided no more than momentary comfort. Soon a new bout of pains came on. They had started to come now in waves, each set stronger than the ones before.

Mabel forced herself to get up. She waddled through to the bathroom. She suddenly had the hope that perhaps it was really that simple. But when she sat on the toilet and pushed nothing came out. Something felt terribly wrong: the wrong sensations coming back to her with each slow groaning push she allowed herself to make.

She put her hand between her legs to check herself again. She felt more deeply this time, her own nail scratching her flesh as she slid her finger in as far as it would go, till she touched upon the obstruction she had already half-expected to find.

And yet, though she touched it, though she pressed her fingertip to it, she didn't quite feel it. She could feel the push of it against her but not her own push against it. It didn't feel as though it was really part of her at all. It felt frighteningly un-her.

In a kitchen drawer she found a large slotted spoon. She had never used it for cooking but it had a long, smooth, brushed-steel handle. Slowly Mabel fed the cool metal of the handle into herself till she could feel its dull tip pressing against the obstruction.

She worked the handle around, trying to dislodge the object, trying to find an edge. She knew that if she could get this thing out of her then she could ease the pain. She also knew that her own pushing upwards against the object didn't hurt, neither with her fingers nor with the metal handle. So she applied more pressure, little by little, till something at length gave way.

It happened suddenly, as though the handle of the slotted spoon had punched straight through a substance as flimsy as paper, and now there was no longer any resistance.

Mabel stopped pushing. Slowly she withdrew the long handle of the spoon. But something else came with it. She felt it as a sudden warmth. A sudden emptying.

There was a gush. A thick wetness. Mabel looked to her feet. She saw the gloopy spatter of red against the white kitchen tiles, a slick of grey mucus spreading out around it.

·

Mabel felt as though she'd been stabbed hard in the gut.

She had never before been stabbed, yet she knew in the very instant of that terrifying moment that this was what being stabbed must feel like.

It wasn't just the sharpness of the jab, nor the sickening pain of her skin being suddenly and so finely divided, it was the deadening sensation of some object that wasn't her being pushed so deeply and so smoothly right inside her.

And it was the shock of her whole body wanting to be rid of this horrible sensation, to pull whatever had entered her out and cast it away, as well as the equally strong desire not to move at all in case any small movement on her part, even breathing, might increase the agony.

•

The room behind the wardrobe was cool and dark. The heating had been shut off but the trays and buckets remained, each holding their dirty residues of water.

The room was cool and dark and it was damp. The air was thick with the scent of creeping mould. Pink and grey and black. The room was exactly where Mabel wanted to be.

The space soothed her. The old couch and its wrinkled leathery skin was homely. She could curl herself up very small here. She could die here. Happily. Comfortably. Condensing back into herself.

Her pains remained, but backgrounded. Her insides were shifting, readjusting.

She closed her eyes.

It was from that low angle, still kneeling on the carpet, that Mabel finally saw him. At least, she saw part of him.

She had been staring towards the bedroom while she steadied herself from the shock of that first stab of pain. The lights were off, but she could see something down by the base of the bed itself, something sticking out from beside it: two black-socked feet.

Mabel crawled forward a short way. Carefully she unbent herself into standing. Then still more warily she hobbled into the bedroom, clutching uselessly at the ache in her belly.

She saw now that not only his feet but the rest of his body lay squidged between the bed and the near wall. He appeared to be lying face down.

Mabel went to crouch, to shake him by his trouser cuff, or by his upturned heel. But bending forward even slightly gave her that same sharp pain. It came on just as suddenly, as intensely, as before, and once again she doubled up.

•

Even lying flat out, stilled and cooled in the mould-scented darkness, the pains did not allow Mabel to rest, and now as they returned they came in force. They multiplied, heaping themselves together.

Mabel wanted nothing more of this. She wanted it to end. She wanted to die. If she could manage it she wanted to reach her hand in deep and rip out all her innards, to turn her own body inside out, expelling herself from herself.

But she made no such attempt. She hadn't the strength. Her face ached. Her bones ached. Her thighs ached. In trying to get to her feet she half-slipped half-tumbled from the couch.

She began to crawl. She didn't know where she was going. Nothing helped. Nowhere was there a haven from the pain.

She got only as far as the corner of the room. She clawed herself upwards, her fingernails dragging at the slippery wallpaper as she tried to stand, as she tried to turn about. But standing was too much, and at length she sank wearily into a squatting position.

She stopped then, for the squatting seemed to offer a small degree of comfort, her insides relaxing to this new gravitational arrangement. But the posture wasn't stable, she still rocked unsteadily on her feet. So Mabel braced her arms and elbows against the wall to support herself, trying to hold position.

And then, because it felt natural to do so, because at that moment she thought she could somehow extend this brief feeling of relief, she took a deep breath, puffing herself with air, before clamping her jaw shut to hold that air in place; the tightness of her teeth to cage in the pressure. It brought the pain back, rising to its peak, but Mabel held it. She held that pain at breaking point, at splitting point. And then, holding it, controlling it, she pushed.

•

This time Mabel didn't fall. She grabbed at the edge of the bed to steady herself.

She no longer cared about trying to wake the body on the floor. She only wanted to get out of there. But as she turned to go something caught her eye. Pale green in the centre of the bed. A tiny rumple of cloth. In reaching for it there came another stab. It sprang like electrical current along her outstretched arm. She still had the old passbook clutched in her hand. She thrust both it and the rescued triangle of green cloth into the pocket of her jacket.

She needed to get out. Out of that stuffy, cramped, dismal little basement flat. She needed to be home, amongst her own grottiness, her own stale smells. She made for the door and hobbled up the coarsely carpeted hallway to the stairs beyond.

Pushing out into the cool of the night Mabel tried her best to straighten up, tried her best not to look like she was staggering as she made her way down the street, towards the glimmer of the taxi rank.

•

She felt dizzy. All that pushing. All that tensed breath. Her mind swam. She could see stars. And when she first felt something slip suddenly from her, and heard some small weight falling dull against the floorboards, she didn't look to see what it was. She didn't care what it was. She knew there was more to come. Even if it meant she pushed out her own lungs, all her held-in air flopping out in its pink fleshy bags. Even if she was left as an empty sack, a raggedy twitch of skin, it didn't matter, so long as that meant it was over.

She took more breath, pumping herself up once again, fighting against the swimming sleepiness that threatened to overwhelm her. Another flop. Another sudden release. And with each release her own sense of relief, slowly deepening.

She could feel the pulpy wetness piling up between her feet. It pressed against her ankles, drying in the air, its tacky softness half-sticking itself to her skin.

She knew when there was nothing left, when all she could push at now was an emptiness, a lack, when she herself had been all but hollowed out.

She allowed herself then to sink down, onto her hands and knees, managing to crawl just a little way forward, away from the corner of the room, till at last, with all the strength gone utterly from her, she lay down flat, with the roughness, the coolness, of the floorboards against her cheek.

28. Going Back

Sal was nearing home.

He had been walking slowly through the outer streets of town, his hands deep in the pockets of his coat. His head was bowed, his eyes fixed downward, watching the steady progress of his feet.

And now the space around him was softening out, becoming that little bit more familiar: the uneven paving slabs his shoes automatically adjusted to; chips in the high kerbstone that marked an unvoiced countdown to his own front door.

He had simply walked, without looking, without caring, and the streets had aligned themselves to bring him here. And now this was his own street, the one he'd lived in all his life—at least till recently.

And yes, that recent shift had brought with it the sense of a new and different place, one he'd also begun to think of as home. But it was a false feeling. It was illusory. It hadn't the deep strength of sensation as this his real home. He'd always be safe here. He could always come back here.

And there would be Madox, old father Madox, as stable and unchanging as ever. Beyond those walls he'd be waiting. He'd be sleeping, which was itself a sort of waiting. He'd wake to find his boy returned and he'd say nothing. He'd accept the normality of Sal's presence and so adjust himself accordingly.

And if Sal didn't come home? Then that waiting would simply be extended. Sal had his own key. His room would be made up, ready for him to return to. And it was his room. His very own. He could burrow back into it. Curl up inside it. He could sleep there without fear or worry or thought for anything except the coming of the next day and the regular contentment of his routine walk to work, his hours of useful labour, his coming home again.

Now the space in which Sal walked began to thin. It was still familiar, still his space, but it was funnelling him outwards, away from the safety of his home. Without noticing, he'd walked right past his front door and on into a street that now, as it came to its end, ceased to have the sense of being part of town.

The pavement tapered off into a flatness, which spread, becoming rough hard earth, earth that began to rise, began to be hillside. And there was the damp mud-patched grass. And there was the winding path, each shallow step reinforced with odd bits of wood.

Sal didn't hesitate. He'd already wandered all night, he could wander a little more. The slope wasn't difficult so long as he took it slowly. And when he reached the slippery-seated bench, with the dark of the scrubby copse behind, he turned and slumped himself onto its wetness.

His hands were still in his pockets. He was cold but he didn't care. Out there now was the whole sleeping town before him. Such a grand complexity of tall tight buildings and little lights. A hazy glowing dome rose over it, reaching up into the thickness of the night sky. And beyond it, far away in the distance on either side, were further glows, small patches of yellowy light that settled on the underside of clouds.

Other towns. Towns like this one, perhaps. Sal had no idea. He had never visited them. His life was here. No reason to leave it. But Mabel would be out there. Somewhere. He didn't need to know where. Maybe that patch of light. Maybe the other. But there she'd be. Sleeping for now. Untroubled. At the very beginning of her new life.

If Sal met her again someday she'd be changed. New clothes. New haircut. New style completely. He might not even recognise her. But she'd know him. He'd be the same as he always was, as he always would be.

More likely he'd never bump into her at all. Because he'd never go to those other towns. And she'd never come back to this one. But she'd be happy. That was surely all that mattered. And Sal could always come up to this hillside and look out over the land, and simply imagine her being somewhere, imagine her being happy. No longer any upsets. No reason to worry. A new contentment. A new way to live.

Sal tried to conjure a picture of when he'd last seen her. It had only been a glimpse: when she'd rushed out into the taxi. She hadn't seen him, of course. She hadn't been thinking of him at that moment. Not in any way. He pushed the memory aside.

He went back further. She'd accepted his scarf, his little gifts. She'd been delighted by them, by him. But she'd been packing. She didn't really have him on her mind. No, not that memory either.

There was their last walk home together. Side by side. Her easy chat. His awkward kiss. And then she'd dismissed him. Just like that. He didn't want to linger on the matter.

His guarding of her, then? All the days spent near her pupal form. Dormant. Unalive. There'd been a sense of true closeness during that time. A sense of responsibility, of care. Except she'd never asked for his protection, hadn't even known him to be there.

But now all this was reaching too far back. Sal couldn't stretch his simple mind to find the sort of memory he needed. Nothing would do. Everything about her within these last few weeks had been pushing towards one thing. Sal had only been a brief unnecessary feature of a much longer plan.

Perhaps then it was a good thing not to have a recent memory of her. A good thing she gently pushed him away and hadn't shared with him where she was going. A good thing he didn't catch up to her at the taxi. What could he have said if he had? She was all ready to go. In the very process of leaving. It would have made things even more awkward. He couldn't very well have—

Sal stood suddenly.

His small black eyes stared hard out over the town. He had a new image in his head. A little moving scene. He replayed it over and over, straining to check all the details.

She had run from the building and got into the taxi.

She hadn't loitered. The taxi hadn't been waiting. Sal had watched as it passed him. It had stopped and she'd got in. She'd got in without any difficulty. She'd got in without her cases.

Her cases. They were still at her apartment. She wasn't leaving that night. She'd never said she was leaving that night. She couldn't have left.

She was still here.

Sal ran down the hill. He ran very fast, faster than was safe, the slope pulling his small weight onward, his shoes hitting hard into the earth. If he slipped and fell he knew he would hurt himself badly, but he didn't make any effort to slow his speed, he couldn't permit this little chance, this tiny vague hope, to disappear. He didn't know what might come of it. He didn't know if it was good. But here it was, in this moment, and now he was running, with all his might, to meet it.

The first glows of dawn were filtering through the newspaper-covered window, through the peeling and curling layers of print, giving a new soft yellowy light to the room where Mabel knelt, her body upright, hands limp in her lap, her damp hair sticking in strands to her forehead and cheeks.

The eggs were globular and white. Their skins had not yet hardened, retaining a milky mistiness, the very faintest of pinks showing through from their insides.

They were in a small uneven pile, cemented together by a foam of grey mucus. Each egg was the size of a clenched fist. There were eight in all, plus a small sag of that same misty white that might have been a ninth, though all that now remained of it was a wrinkle of broken shell.

Mabel placed the flat of her hand against her belly. Her pain was wholly different now. It felt much deeper. It was a pain of sickening emptiness. As though there was a huge hole in her middle that the rearrangement of her insides could not fill, every organ straining at their strings as they hung down into it. A residue of tension ran through her muscles, a slow aching spasm, her body still wanting weakly to push, but with nothing left now to come out.

Slowly Mabel rose to her feet and left the room. The wardrobe had been stripped of most of its contents, the old coats and jackets and dresses lying in a heap beyond it. Mabel left both doorways open as she stepped through.

In the bathroom she filled the basin with hot water, waiting till the rising surface began to slip backward down the overflow. She reduced the tap to a trickle, keeping the water in continuous renewal, the gurgle of the run-off never ceasing.

Mabel checked herself over. She slipped from her yellow skirt and gently sponged the inside of her legs. Pink-tinted water pooled at her feet and soaked into the carpet. She ignored it, shifting herself to stand in a dry spot when she was done.

Unbuttoning her pale blue blouse Mabel examined the tenderness she could still feel in her belly. But there was nothing for her to see. The pains were all internal. They would settle eventually. She stepped back into her skirt, rebuttoned her blouse and tucked herself in. The blue silk had gone purple under her arms. Salt-streaks showed at the edges of each stain. She let that be for now. It wouldn't be visible once her striped jacket was on.

Mabel gazed at herself in the mirror. Her hair appeared darker. It had taken on a reddish tinge. No longer was there any sign of that beautiful golden lustre. The hair fell lank and lifeless. It felt greasy to the touch.

Her eyes too had lost some of their brilliant blueness. They'd darkened at their edges. Their middles now looked green. Mabel squinted. Perhaps it was no more than an illusion brought on by the strip bulb over the mirror, its soft fluorescent glow.

Mabel rinsed and combed her hair. She washed her face. She turned off the tap and pulled the cord for the light.

Her two cases lay open on the bed, her new clothes already neatly folded, arranged and pressed inside. She checked them, idly thumbing through layers of fabric, counting as she went. Among the items were three more skirts, each the same cut as the one she was wearing but differently coloured. After a moment's consideration Mabel changed into one that was chequered in grey and black. The soiled yellow skirt she rolled up tightly, stuffing it into a sealable inner compartment.

There was still plenty of space in the cases if she needed it. She glanced around the room, at the heap of oddments by the wardrobe, at the damp towels on the floor of the bathroom, at the cheap misshapen cushions on the couch.

Beside the bed was her small radio. She unplugged it from the wall, collapsed its aerial, wound its thin brown flex around it, and nestled it into the centre of the case that was marginally less full. Then, having rearranged the clothes still further, she cinched the inner straps tight and zipped both cases closed.

Mabel stood a moment reflecting. Her railway ticket was still in its long envelope inside her jacket. She could feel its top edge gently digging into her. She took it out, checked its validity, checked the destination, and carefully put the envelope back in her pocket.

The cases weren't heavy. One had a long strap, enabling Mabel to loop it over her shoulder to hang at her back.

The other she could transfer from left grip to right, if such a need arose.

Joggling her keys in one hand she gave the room a last lookover in case there was anything obvious she was forgetting, then she dropped the keys into the empty fruitbowl on the counter and turned towards the door. She undid the two chains and opened up, the suitcase on her back bumping awkwardly against the jamb as she angled herself through the gap.

She stopped. The building around her felt uncommonly quiet. It made her own small noises all the more prominent. She stood for a moment in the doorway, listening.

There was nothing. The building still slept.

Mabel tightened her jaw. She set off down the hall with a sure and steady step, her gaze fixed firmly forward. Behind her she heard the soft click of her front door falling closed.

Sal stood in the dimly-lit corridor. His little heart thumped loudly, shushing its fluids up around his ears. The sensation dizzied him. His legs were suffused with an overwhelming weakness. He felt too hot in his old coat. He felt sick.

The building around him buzzed. A constant low vibration. It made the air seem hazy—Sal's small black eyes now struggling in the thin grey light the growing dawn permitted into the building.

The apartment door wasn't locked. It swung back easily at his push. As he went through the buzzing swelled around him. It began to pulse. Sal blinked his eyes tightly.

The room was in a state. There was a damp smell in the air. A dark stain stood out stark against the plain white tiles of the kitchen floor. The stain had congealed. It glistened as Sal crouched to inspect it more closely. He put out his fingers to touch it then drew back.

A thin trail led away from the stain. Further small dark spatters. There was a slotted spoon with a long metal handle lying on the carpet. Sal bent to pick it up. He gripped it tightly in his little fist as he followed the drip-trail up to and through the open wardrobe.

The light inside the room was a soft yellow-grey. It still seemed dim. Sal could see dark speckles before his eyes that swam and shifted wherever he looked. He tried to calm his breathing by shutting his mouth, letting the air hiss faintly through his nose.

The clutch of eggs at the room's corner had a pale glow all of their own. Sal knelt close beside them. He reached out. He touched them. The eggs had a nacreous lustre. Their smoothness made them feel wet. They seemed slippery.

Their shells had not yet fully hardened. When Sal pressed against the side of an egg with the tip of the spoon's handle he found he could make a small dent in that otherwise rounded surface. And then, as Sal drew back, the egg slowly undented itself, resuming its perfect curve.

When Sal pressed just a little harder the long blunt handle of the slotted spoon broke through the soft white shell. It pushed in easily, with no more than a gentle popping sensation, making not a sound. And in withdrawing the handle so the inside of the egg spilled out, elongating its dark red yolk as it ran down over the other shells, splitting and spreading smoothly onto the floorboards.

Sal pressed against more eggs, in just the same way as before. It was so very easy. It required neither thought nor any special effort. Each egg slowly sagged as it was punctured, as its insides leaked and split and joined with the spread of the other eggs.

Till Sal knelt looking at the beautiful mess he'd made. The flop of thick white shells. The long dark ripples of red amid the misty slick as it dried, as it formed a second skin, coagulating while Sal watched.

Sal put down the slotted spoon. He stood to leave. But in glancing again towards the corner he saw there was one egg he'd missed. It looked that much more rounded now, among the floppy ruins of its siblings. It looked out of place.

Crouching this time Sal placed his hands around it. It was warm. He squeezed it, gently, but its skin was not as giving as the others had been, or else Sal's fingers didn't have the same hard strength as the handle of the spoon. Instead, as Sal squeezed, the egg abruptly came loose from its hardened grey base.

And as the egg broke off so Sal lost his balance, stumbling backward as he tried to straighten, slipping in the pinkish slick of yolk. But, though he wobbled and staggered and slid, he managed not to fall.

Sal stood firm, breathing hard once again through his nose, the egg held safe before him. It fitted so neatly between his blue-grey hands. It nestled even more perfectly in the fleecy inside pocket of his coat. It would hardly be noticeable from without, though he could feel the small bulge of it pressing against him as he hurried from the room. He almost tripped on leaving the apartment. He didn't stop to check if the door fell closed. But he'd calmed a little by the time he stepped outside.

The morning was cold, much colder than the night. But Sal was warm in his coat. He walked with his hands pushed deep in his pockets. If anyone was to see him now they'd never guess what he carried. To them he'd look perfectly normal. He'd look just like anyone else.

31. A MORNING CALL

When Inspector Augustine woke he found himself wedged between the bed and the wall. It was a tight space. He couldn't think how he'd ended up there. He felt exhausted.

His memory of the previous evening was full of holes. He recalled waiting for Mabel at a restaurant but not the moment of her arrival. He could remember eating but not what it was he ate. After that things became still more hazy. He had his suspicions. He tried to push them away—he'd always thought of himself as more cautious than that.

On finding the yellow-green scarf draped carelessly over the back of an armchair the inspector guessed more fully at what had happened. He bunched the cheap fabric to his nose and sniffed it. The scent was weak but it was enough to make him swoon once again. He clutched the back of the chair for a moment, his sight first fading into a swirl of reds before swimming painfully back in a rushing checkerboard of blues and greys.

He went to get a drink of water. An unwashed tumbler stood beside the sink. He gulped down three glasses then headed calmly for the front door, collecting his long leather coat on the way and pushing the crumpled scarf down into a pocket.

It was still early morning. The streets were not busy. Augustine drove with the windows down, letting the cold air stream in. He slowed when he spied pedestrians up ahead, taking a good look at each one as he drew near. But they were nothing more than larvals. They were nobodies.

·

Augustine parked directly outside Mabel's building. Yet another old larval stood staring at him as he entered. She smiled at the inspector as he passed by. The inspector ignored her.

The apartment door wasn't closed. An obstruction prevented it from shutting completely, a creased and edgeworn pamphlet. Augustine nudged the object aside with his foot. He glanced briefly round the room then headed for the wardrobe. He attempted to shift the whole thing to one side before noticing the false back. He took a small torch from his pocket. He twisted out its thin beam and stepped on through.

He saw the dried up rumple of skin on the couch. He saw the destroyed clutch of eggs in the opposite corner. Neither surprised him. He swallowed hard, then went to the window and, getting his fingernails under the layers of newspaper, peeled most of it away in one long careful motion.

He crouched by the broken eggs. He reached out a hand to the slick of red yolk, dragging his fingertips over the glossy surface, testing its consistency. Only a thin skin had yet formed. It rucked easily, breaking at his touch.

From inside his coat the inspector took a small silver camera. Moving out of the path of light coming in from the window he took several shots of the broken eggs from different angles, slowly winding on the film between each frame, feeling the soft rasp of the ratchet beneath his thumb.

There were footprints in the mess of yolk. He photographed these as well, using his torch this time to create appropriate shadow. He measured the footprints, noting the details in his pocketbook. He counted the remaining shells. From a smooth indentation in the grey crust he could see that one of the eggs was missing. He measured this indentation, making a note of that too.

Lastly he took out a small roll of plastic bags, tore one off, and with it picked up the discarded spoon, inverting the bag around the implement and sealing it inside.

Back in the main room he found a set of keys. These he also bagged. Then, with a last glance round, he left, pulling the door now firmly closed behind him.

•

Down in the entrance hall Inspector Augustine stood leaning against the wall beside the payphone, its bulky receiver tucked into his neck. He gazed through the building's glass frontage, absentmindedly counting the dial tones as they rang. The day outside was growing, strong and bright.

Getting no reply after fifteen rings the inspector straightened, took a deep breath, and hung up. His coin clattered through the machine and he retrieved it.

For a moment he stood, staring through the window at his car parked neatly on the road outside. Then, lifting the receiver once more, he dropped the coin back in the slot and dialled a different number.